Judex: Ceige and Sloane

Zahra Delsine

Northshore Noir Press

Northshore Noir Press
Toronto, Canada
www.northshorenoir.com

ISBN: 978-1-998648-07-8

eBook ISBN: 978-1-998648-08-5

For more information visit: northshorenoir.com

Contents

Chapter 1

The frost bites.

Teeth in the air, knives on the wind.

Cryosium doesn't just kill you, Ceige Rivers thinks. It devours you.

She crouches on the edge of a rooftop, perched like a bird of prey. Night stretches below, a frozen labyrinth of jagged ice and shadow. Cryosium—city of the damned, where breath turns to ghost vapor and danger whispers from every corner.

But at this moment? There's only him.

Viktor Volkov.

Ceige's eyes narrow as a figure skirts through the alleyway below. Shadows cling to him like frost to glass, but she knows it's him—she's seen the mark stitched onto his jacket. That emblem—Syndicate black and silver. A badge for men who believe they own this city.

No one owns Cryosium. Not even Judex like Ceige. They operate above the law but beneath its shadow, a necessary contradiction in a city where justice is bought and sold. When the courts fail and the powerful slip through their grasp, the Judex step in—investigators, executioners, and the last line of consequence. There are no juries, no appeals, just swift judgment.

She's heard people speak their name in hushed tones, watched them struggle between fear and reverence. But the truth is simple: the Judex don't uphold justice. They maintain balance, one body at a time.

"Let's see what you've got," Ceige mutters, her breath curling into the air.

The wind churns as she moves. A single push off the ledge sends her descending into shadows. Her boots hit snow soundlessly—enhanced bones fine-tuning every motion with precision only science could buy. Twisted genetics, they call it. A gift or a curse, depending on who you ask. For Ceige? It's survival.

Every step resonates—snow crunching sharply beneath her weight, ice glinting treacherously under powder-light covering. She flows through it all with the ease of someone molded by this frozen wasteland; instincts keen as a blade sliding into place. The world feels alive to her—each gust of wind stinging like a lover's bite, each echo ricocheting down Cryosium's skeletal streets filling her mapless mind with coordinates of potential death.

A laugh drifts faintly from some distant bar. Ghostly joy in a city that bleeds misery.

"All according to plan," she murmurs, lips curling bitter-sweet around the cliche.

Her prey emerges from darkness: Viktor "Frostbite" Volkov steps into pale streetlight like an actor hitting his mark, flanked by two hulking shadows masquerading as bodyguards. Arrogance rolls off him—a heat illusion in this frigid nightscape—but it doesn't thaw him out. Nothing in Cryosium burns long enough to stay warm. He wears his power heavy on his shoulders, oblivious that he's already been marked for death.

Her gloved fingers delve into her pack without hesitation. Methodical movements; no wasted effort. One item after another emerges under moonlight's pale gaze: tools honed by necessity and perfected by time. A custom sidearm nestles in her grip like an extension of herself—the barrel gleaming silver-cold under Cryosium's half-dead sky.

Frost-resistant rounds clink softly as they slide into place one by one. Deadly precision forged for a world where heat is fleeting and failure leaves blood frozen in its tracks.

Perfect fit.

And then: the picks. Twin blades folded sleekly against themselves until her hands coax them open with a soft metallic hiss. They catch what little light exists—razor edges gleaming like fangs carved from winter itself.

Sharp enough to sever flesh and splinter bone.

Good.

Her lips curl—part grin, part snarl—as she slips the weapons back into their sheathes with reverence earned through years of use.

Enough prep work.

The detachment settles over her again without invitation or effort—a shroud worn too long to ever be discarded fully. Emotions are excess weight; judgment cannot afford indulgences like fear or fury here in this frozen labyrinth, where missteps mean death.

She straightens slowly, every movement deliberate as steel cables pulled taut between anchor points.

The frost bit.

Sharp teeth, cold breath.

Ice in the air, ice in her veins.

Ceige watches from cover and lines up her gun—a perfect extension of herself, its weight familiar in her hands like an old lover returned after years apart.

The world shrinks to this moment—the rhythm of her breath matching the pulse of her heart, matching the stillness of winter itself. Time freezes as sharp as Cryosium's air; even sound seems brittle, ready to break at any moment under pressure.

"Goodbye," she whispers finally, savoring the icy resolve that settles over her bones.

Her finger tightens on the trigger.

The silenced shot slips through the night like a secret carried on the wind. Viktor staggers forward once—twice—and then collapses into himself: a marionette cut free from its strings.

His guards turn too late—their confusion hangs heavy in their wide eyes, pale faces caught between disbelief and fear.

"Too slow." Her voice drips mockery as she slides back into the cold embrace of shadow and snow—the only allies she has ever trusted.

Her heart thuds hard against bone—not fear, but thrill; not survival, but triumph. Somewhere above Cryosium's endless graveyard streets, another sin is erased by blood and a fee.

She disappears as easily as frost melting under brief sunbeams—but Cryosium doesn't notice or care.

It never does.

Ceige's heart drums.

A relentless rhythm in her chest.

The hunt is done, but the game? The game never ends.

Preparation is survival. And survival is everything.

She drops into an alley—narrow, suffocating, its frost-slick walls squeezing inward like ribs closing around a heart—and kneels on the brittle ground.

All according to plan, Ceige, she tells herself. Just another night. The words feel hollow in her head, but she says them anyway because habit has its comforts.

Cryosium is hers tonight—a playground carved from ice and quiet death—and she knows its rules better than anyone else.

Ceige presses her back against the brick wall. It gnaws through her jacket, the rough edges scraping at her skin. Cryosium thuds around her—cars streaking by like silver bullets, a faint burst of laughter fractured by distance, the low hum of a world grinding on without pause. The blood in the snow hasn't had time to freeze, and yet here they are—oblivious. It never ceases to claw at her. How easily life continues as if death isn't threading its way through the cracks.

"Time to disappear," she murmurs, barely louder than the hiss of escaping breath. Her eyes sweep the street, seeking the glint of watchful lenses or curious stares. But no one ever truly sees her. She is a shadow in Cryosium's frozen veins, a ghost leaving only silence behind.

Tonight isn't any different.

She exhales once and pushes off the wall. Sliding into the darkness between pools of pale light, she moves like smoke peeling from a dying fire—indistinct, unstoppable. Then she sees it: a flicker of silver cutting through the dark—a camera. Its eye gleams under weak streetlights like polished steel catching moonlight. Ceige drops low without thought, knees skimming frost-slicked pavement as she melts into the shadows.

The camera moves slowly, its glassy gaze sweeping back and forth across the alleyway. Ceige doesn't move. Doesn't breathe. Tension coils tight in her chest like a wound spring ready to snap.

"Away," she mutters under her breath, fingers twitching against her thigh as impatience gnaws at her resolve. "Look away."

The lens gives way at last, turning its attention elsewhere. Ceige is already moving before it completes its arc, sliding out from her hiding spot with an ease born of repetition. Her breath pushes out in a cold plume as relief washes over her, sharp-edged and fleeting.

No mistakes tonight.

Turn after turn pulls her deeper into Cryosium's frozen labyrinth—iron grates crusted with ice; alleys too narrow for light to follow; walls that close tighter with each step until they feel alive, pressing against her ribs like breathless panic given form. Somewhere below this city sprawls the Underground Network—a place where secrets bloom thick as ice crystals on cracked windows—and Ceige flits toward it like wind slicing through brittle branches.

She is untouchable tonight, a specter gliding through Cryosium's icy skin. Death's companion cloaked in frost and whispers, leaving nothing but silence behind.

And she loves it.

"Onward," she murmurs with something close to laughter catching in her throat—a sound swallowed quickly by cold air as it leaves her lips. Onward to whatever comes next. This is hers, this empty existence—sharp-edged and solitary—and there isn't much left that can challenge that claim.

The alley narrows again beneath jagged rooftops jutting out above like skeletal fingers reaching for stars that aren't there anymore. Frost clings to every crack and corner; Ceige's boots crunch against it as she moves forward without hesitation. Her breath curls into thin ribbons that rise only to dissolve into nothingness above her head.

This frozen graveyard is alive in its own way—a dead thing refusing burial—and Ceige revels in it. That hum beneath it all matches hers now: steady, relentless purpose thrumming hard through veins laced with adrenaline and ice-cold clarity.

She turns a corner sharply—and then stops dead at the sound of something breaking its silence:

Ping.

It vibrates against her thigh like an aftershock pulsing up from deep below ground—a burst of noise too sharp for this quiet void to contain comfortably. Ceige reaches down reflexively and pulls out the secure comm device buried beneath layers of thermal camouflage. Its screen glows faintly blue against white-knuckled fingers trembling slightly—not from nerves but anticipation barely held at bay.

Her gaze slides over two words etched across pale light:

Eira Halstead.

For a moment—it is brief but heavy—the name hangs there between bloodless fingers and frostbitten air before slamming into Ceige's mind like shattering glass scattering across ice sheets slick enough already with danger's familiar weight pressing down everywhere all at once.

Halstead?

Her stomach twists—not fear exactly but something sharper; curiosity steeped too long until bitter—and unease curls tight alongside it before either can fully settle or explain themselves away entirely.

"Fuck me," Ceige mutters softly.

The city moans its encouragement.

Cryosium sighs under the weight of its own desires.

The device glows.

A faint, cold light.

It washes over Ceige's face as she studies the dossier. Eira Halstead—microbiologist, philanthropist, civic leader. A name written on a ledger, now reduced to a target.

Her finger traces the blueprints glowing on the tablet screen. Lines, doors, checkpoints—she maps them like arteries in a body, plotting where to cut.

Surveillance photos flicker into view. The third-shift guards move along their routes, night after night. Predictable patterns, easy to exploit. One guard sneaks out to the loading dock at 2:00 AM for his cigarette—always at 2:00 AM. But something scratches at the back of her mind—an itch she can't quite reach. The camera angles are too clean, too precise. Recently captured.

Someone else has been watching.

Ceige pinches and zooms on a corner of the blueprint—the maintenance door in the basement lab. There it is. A single charge placed there would do it. The alarms would scream through the building like wounded animals. Security would flood the labs in a panicked wave, leaving the residential wing wide open.

Leaving Eira exposed.

Her finger hovers over "accept." The money is good—too good. The kind you don't turn down unless you're tired of breathing. And just enough to draw out competition like flies to blood. She knows she isn't the only one with these blueprints burned into her mind, these patterns memorized step by step.

But she'll be the one to finish it.

Before she can do accept, another ping. This one for Sloane Vale. A rival Judex. But the fee for her death is low, far too low for anyone capable of killing her. Ceige toys with the idea of accepting the job.

"She must've pissed someone off," Ceige mutters to no one, rolling a shoulder stiffened by hours in the cold. Her voice is swallowed by the stillness, but the ghosts hear it anyway—they always do.

Ceige's grin sharpens—predatory, cold—and a glint of mischief sparks in her icy-blue eyes. This job won't come easy, but there's no thrill in easy work. No satisfaction in clean hands.

This will be a glorious mess.

She presses "accept" and watches as the device purges itself, erasing every trace of the contract, as if it had never existed at all. Ceige dismantles the comm methodically, her hands moving without thought or hesitation, while her mind runs ahead to choreograph her ploy:

The blast like thunder tearing through stone. Guards scrambling down corridors in a useless stampede. Seconds stretching thin like thread as Halstead's apartment lies unguarded and open to her bullet.

One shot.

One exit.

Nothing left behind but silence.

Ceige scatters the pieces of the device in separate trash bins as she walks away from the safety of shadows into something colder and sharper—resolve.

Someone else is hunting Halstead; she knows that now with certainty.

Snow drifts like ash, settling over crooked alleyways and deadened streets. Ceige feels the pulse beneath her boots, the faint thrum of life stirring in its frozen veins. She scans the empty road ahead, but she knows better—Cryosium never sleeps.

It watches.

Eyes linger behind frost-coated windows. Whispers curl around darkened corners. The ghosts here don't rest, and tonight, they're laughing at her.

Another single ping breaks the silence—this time her phone—vibrating against her palm. The fee notification slides onto her device, glowing cold as the air around her. A half-smirk tugs at her lips.

She maps it out in her head—threading herself into Eira's world like a silver needle through silk. Ceige doesn't mind waiting for cracks to form—patience is another blade in her arsenal, honed alongside a relentless resolve she wears like steel armor.

Her steps crunch soft and steady over the snow-blanketed street. Eyes forward. Thoughts sharper now than ever before.

A pair of drunks slump against a doorway up ahead—unmoving shadows against an uneven wall—but they're nothing to her. Just echoes of lives forgotten by this city built on chaos and silence, collateral swept aside without a second thought.

She moves past them without hesitation.

Her focus won't falter—not now—not with Eira fixed so firmly in her sights.

Chapter 2

The streets of Cryosium shiver.

Ice and shadow, frozen ghosts.

Ceige moves like a whisper through the city's veins, her breath trailing behind her in pale wisps that vanish into the cold. The night is vast and heavy, pressing down on her, swallowing every sound but the crunch of snow beneath her boots. Ahead, a building rises from the darkness—faceless, unremarkable. Its windows are black and empty. Dead eyes cannot see her reconnaissance.

Eiskorps. A name wrapped in satin sharp as broken glass. Tonight, Ceige plans to tear it open and see what bleeds.

Ceige wants to know why someone wants Eira dead. By all accounts she is a kind-hearted champion of the downtrodden blah, blah, blah. It is almost always a cover for something. But Ceige like to know the why, if she can. Like a cop who wants a confession: unnecessary but desirable.

A dumpster looms in the alley. Ceige slips behind it, presses her back against its frozen steel skin. The cold bites through her coat, wicked and alive, but the sting grounds her—it tells her she's still breathing. Still here.

The wind weeps down the narrow street, cutting across her exposed cheek like a blade. She doesn't flinch, only waits, body taut as wire as her eyes sweep for movement. The street is still.

Ceige makes her way to the back of Eiskorps, and waits.

A flicker of light arcs through the air as the guard flicks his cigarette, its glowing embers snuffed out in the snow. The loading dock door groans as it begins closing behind him.

Just as she hopes, he turns away.

Tick, tick, tick.

With a lunge, she darts across the open ground and slides through the gap before the door's edge can cut her in two.

Inside: dim light and the sound of retreating footsteps. The guard is going back to whatever the fuck it is that guards do.

Shadows crawl along the walls, twisting into shapes that clutch at her with finger-like edges—hungry things left too long in this place. The air hangs stale around her face, thick with dust and something faintly metallic. Blood? No—just neglect.

Each step is a dance on thin ice. Ceige moves without sound, fluid as water frozen midstream—a body trained to exist in treachery and not be consumed by it. This is the game she knows best: move light, stay low.

It feels familiar now—the coiled tension deep in her gut that tightens with every step down this long corridor. A presence almost comforting in its constancy. Her heartbeat quickens—not fear but anticipation sparking through her veins like electricity warming dead circuits.

She grins at the absurdity of it all.

"All according to plan," she murmurs to no one but herself, the words slipping from between clenched teeth as white vapor clouds. The hunt doesn't scare her—not anymore. It's what lives inside her during the hunt that rattles like chains: betrayal bleeding into memory; trust shattered like glass underfoot. Ghosts that follow her here even now—reminders of why she fights.

But tonight isn't about ghosts.

It's about verification. Always verify the information.

Her hand brushes the corner of a wall slick with condensation as faint voices slip through cracks in solitude. She freezes there—silent and still—but leans closer until only inches separate her from danger unseen.

Two men speak in hurried tones that twist through the quiet like threads pulled taut from opposite ends. Ceige catches fragments—"Halstead" cutting through like an ax blade; "contract" curling behind it like smoke dissipating into air too thin to hold it.

Eiskorps guards.

"Fuck," she whispers. Not now.

She sinks deeper into the shadows, slipping into their embrace like a second skin. Her breath evens out—controlled, deliberate—as her eyes dart across the room, searching for cracks in the fortress around her. Vulnerabilities. Weaknesses.

Then she sees it. A flicker in the dark.

A door leaking whispers of light from the soft glow of computer screens inside. The glow crawls through the space between tile and metal. An invitation she can't ignore. Or maybe a trap, she thinks.

Ceige doesn't hesitate. She's there in three strides, crossing the space like a phantom. Her fingers hover above the entry keys, trembling—not with fear but with hunger. There's something here; she feels it in her bones, senses the weight of it pressing against her skin. Information waiting to be unearthed, raw and dangerous.

She knows the 'why' lives in that room.

"What do you have for me?" she murmurs, her voice threading through the silence like smoke. She's ready to tear into this place, to rip out its truth and devour it whole.

But then—footsteps.

One step. Another.

The sharp rhythm cuts through the quiet and slices through her nerves like a blade. Someone is out there. Coming closer.

Her heart slams against her ribcage—once, twice—then falls into time with those footsteps. She spins away from the door and melts back into the shadows, pulse hammering in her throat like a warning drum.

Stealth.

Precision.

Control.

She crouches low behind the desk, every muscle taut as a wire about to snap, and aims toward the door.

The footsteps recede and disappear.

On hands and knees she crawls back to the door.

Dim and pale, the light from under the door reflects against the polished floor, across Ceige's face, shadowing the lines etched by too many long nights and close calls. Her X-9 hums softly, the vibration slipping into her bones as if the tool were part of her. The pen is sleek, deadly in its subtlety—a scalpel to cut through defenses, a whisper to tease out combinations. She presses it to the lock, fingers steady, breath clouding faintly in the cold air.

It resists. It always resists.

"Come on," she murmurs, voice low, coaxing—not pleading. That would be weakness. And Ceige doesn't plead.

The lock surrenders with a soft beep. She nudges the door open, inch by careful inch, and slips inside. Her pulse drums against her ribs as though it doesn't belong to her—wild and reckless, deafening in the stillness. The door clicks shut behind her. She listens for another sound but hears only her own breathing.

Blue light spills from half-dead monitors, painting sharp angles across a room drowning in disarray. Papers scatter like brittle leaves across a scarred desk; some have fallen to the floor as though they gave up trying to keep their secrets hidden. Ceige moves slowly, scanning every corner—a predator circling its prey.

A bomb could live and die here.

Discipline keeps her footsteps silent as she glides toward the desk. Each scrap of paper promises answers but whispers lies instead: contracts filled with empty words, proposals stacked like flimsy shields obscuring truth. She rifles through them methodically—practiced fingers flipping each page like they're nothing more than ghosts of failed leads.

She wonders who marked Eira for death—which loyal friend traded trust for thirty pieces of silver. She mutters under her breath, frustration curling at the edges of her resolve. She needs more information on her target, to understand who she is. Or will no longer be.

Her hand pauses.

An envelope—tucked beneath a haphazard pile of reports—its seal whole and unaddressed. It waits like bait in a trap or treasure forgotten by careless hands. Ceige plucks it free with a sharp motion and tears it open without hesitation.

A flash drive glints inside.

Small but heavy in its significance, it catches what little light there is and throws it back at her—a shard of hope wrapped in cold steel. Ceige slides it between her fingers once before slotting it into a waiting port on one of the flickering monitors. The screen stirs at her intrusion, lines of code cascading down like rain over shattered glass.

Her eyes narrow as she leans closer.

There's something here—buried deep beneath encryption meant to keep scavengers at bay. Words reach out from the chaos like jagged edges threatening to draw blood: 'classified,' 'operation.' Each one drips with weight and meaning that scratches at the walls of Ceige's mind. She knows this feeling too well—it's adrenaline wrapped in unease, a thrill she can't shake but doesn't trust.

Someone wanted her to find this. Was it the client? Or...

Betrayal unlocks the darkest doors with perfect silence.

Everyone's dirty somewhere, she thinks.

Even me.

The smirk fades as quickly as it came because now there are questions gnawing at the edges of her thoughts: Whose hands planted this? Whose secrets are bleeding out onto these screens? The answers twist beneath layers of code too thick to cut through all at once—but they're there.

And so is something else—a shadow creeping just beyond recognition. Ceige sits still for just a moment longer than she should've allowed herself, staring at what she's uncovered but not really seeing it anymore.

The chill comes first.

A cold that cuts deeper than the howling winds outside.

The hairs on Ceige's neck bristle, instincts flaring, primal and sharp. Danger. It presses down on her, silent and suffocating. She doesn't hesitate as she whispers to herself, "Gotta get outta here before someone crashes the unparty."

She turns to leave but falters, thoughts snaring her. The drive—will it piece everything together? Or is it evidence to frame her? Betrayal wears many faces. Faces she's trusted before. The thought lingers like a blade at her back, but there's no time for doubt. The shadows writhe just beyond the doorway, drawing her forward with their empty promise of escape.

She shoves the drive back into the envelope and slips the envelope back into the pile of papers.

Time to go.

Footsteps echo down the corridor behind her—sharp, deliberate sounds that cut through the thick silence like knives. Ceige freezes mid-step, every nerve honed to a razor's edge. Her hand brushes the grip of her weapon—it feels alive under her fingers, an extension of herself. The air around her tightens, heavy and oppressive, as if even the walls are holding their breath in anticipation.

The footsteps close in—slow and too certain. Each one lands with weight that vibrates through her chest and rattles loose a thread of fear she can't quite suppress. Her pulse hums with adrenaline; it floods her veins hot and electric until she can almost taste it—a bitter tang at the back of her throat mixing with frost and dust hanging stale in the air.

She shifts slightly in the shadows, muscles tense, coiled tight enough to spring if she has to fight—or run.

And then it happens—the door bursts open as if struck by lightning itself.

Sloane Vale steps into the room like chaos personified, wild and unrelenting. Her hair tumbles untamed, framing sharp angles softened only by those vivid green eyes—eyes that glint with amusement or malice; Ceige can never tell which. She doesn't belong here in this sterile place of quiet and frost; Sloane is a storm ripping through order itself.

"Well," Sloane says, voice curling low and sharp as a blade dragged slow across glass, "look who decided to go ninja in my domain." Her smirk pulls wide—a wolf baring teeth—and even though sarcasm drips from every word, it feels like fire delivered straight to Ceige's chest.

Ceige straightens—a deliberate effort masking the racing pulse betraying her calm facade. "Not here for small talk," she says flatly, keeping her tone steady even as heat burns faintly up her neck. She's careful not to let it show—not here, not now—but Sloane always had a way of stirring things best left buried deep beneath ice.

Sloane steps closer, each movement sleek and lethal like a predator circling its prey—not hurried but calculated. The light catches against wild strands of hair as if charged by some unseen storm brewing around her.

"Really?" Sloane tilts her head slightly as if mocking thoughtfulness while pacing closer still. "Because from where I'm standing," she continues smoothly, "it looks an awful lot like you're getting cozy with secrets I'd hate for you to take from me."

She stops just short of closing all distance between them—close enough now that Ceige feels torn between drawing steel or stepping back into shadow—but Sloane only grins wider as if daring either action.

"What's wrong?" Sloane asks softly, voice lilting like silk over broken glass. "Afraid I'll take all the credit?"

The room is cold.

Frigid air bites at Ceige's skin, but it's not the chill that makes her tense—it's *her.*

Sloane moves through the room like a storm rolling in, dark and electric. The walls seem to shudder with her arrival, the faint glow of the flickering light above casting jagged edges across her face.

"You should tread lightly," Ceige says, her voice low, steady as a loaded gun. "This is my job."

Sloane steps closer, slow and deliberate, until the space between them is nothing but a whisper. The scent of smoke and steel clings to her like a second skin. "I'm the one who got paid, sweetheart."

Sweetheart. The word scrapes against Ceige's nerves like flint striking stone, and it sparks something she doesn't want to name.

"You too? Or are you lying?"

Sloane tilts her head, sharp eyes cutting through Ceige's defenses like wire on skin. "Lying of course. I thrive on chaos," she says, soft yet deadly, a blade wrapped in silk. "And this? This place? It's practically begging for me."

Their gazes collide—fire meeting ice. For a moment neither of them moves; the air between them hums, thick and charged, volatile enough to ignite.

Ceige forces herself to hold steady under the weight of those eyes—eyes that burn too intensely, too dangerously. Her resolve frays at the edges as Sloane leans in, close enough the heat rolls off her in waves.

"Nice try," Ceige snaps finally, sharpening her tone into something vicious and cold. She reminds herself why she's here—what matters most: stay focused, stay untouchable. "But I'm not here to play games."

"Who said anything about games?" Sloane's voice drops lower now—taunting yet intimate—and the words slide between them with the precision of a knife sinking into flesh. "This isn't a game, darling. This is survival of the fittest. And I'm very good at surviving."

Darling?

How Disney.

Her smile cuts deep—feral and unrelenting—and before Ceige can react, Sloane leans even closer until their breaths tangle in the dead air around them.

Ceige stiffens as something sharp jolts through her—a live wire dragged across exposed nerves—and she hates that for one fleeting second, she doesn't pull away.

"Get out," she hisses finally, more to herself than to Sloane. Each word feels heavy in her throat—a command weighted down by something she doesn't want to name.

But Sloane doesn't move.

No—the predator stays exactly where she is.

"Make me," she whispers instead—soft as ash falling onto dying embers—with eyes glinting like polished glass hiding all its cracks.

The world narrows then; it shrinks into this suffocating little gap filled with nothing but shadows and heat and barely restrained chaos. There are no walls here—no rules or boundaries left standing upright anymore. It's just them now: two forces locked in this strange gravitational pull toward destruction or something darker still...

"You're playing with fire," Ceige warns through clenched teeth.

Danger coils around every word like smoke winding toward flame.

Heat radiates between them.

A smirk carves across Sloane's lips, sharp as a blade. "I love the way fire burns," she says, her voice low, molten. "Isn't that what we do? Burn the fire itself to ash before it consumes us?"

"Stay out of my way," Ceige replies, but the words fall dead in the frozen air, lifeless and brittle.

Sloane steps closer. The distance shrinks. A breath apart now. Her voice drops to a murmur, a whisper laced with smoke. "Or maybe," she says, each syllable deliberate, the flicker of a flame at Ceige's ear, "we could find a way to ignite together."

The space between them collapses. The icy walls lean inward, suffocating, cold but alive, pressing them toward the edge. Fire and ice wrestling for dominance as they hover above the abyss—desire and danger so tightly wound that one slip would send them plunging into either, or both.

Ceige coils like a spring about to snap. Every nerve tightens; instincts scream. But Sloane doesn't back away. She growls closer, her eyes locked on Ceige's like a predator. The air hums between them—electric, volatile—crackling with unsaid truths and unspoken threats.

Movement.

They circle each other. Silent footsteps shuffling over cold concrete—their arena, their cage.

"I like what they've done to the place." Sloane's voice cuts through the tension like a knife against glass. She gestures lazily toward the cluttered desks piled high with papers and artifacts from another life—a taunt wrapped in velvet sarcasm. A smirk curls at her mouth like smoke rising from embers. "Really suits Eira's...taste."

Ceige glares back through narrowed eyes, her words flat and sharp-edged. "Why are you here, really?" There's venom in her tone but something else beneath it too—a flicker of something reluctant yet undeniable: respect for Sloane's fearless defiance.

"Because."

"You need to be more disciplined," Ceige says as she slides to the left.

"Disciplined." Sloane practically spits the word out, then laughs—a sound that ricochets off the icy walls like shattering glass shards. "Am I being naughty?" Her voice drips derision as she takes another step forward, her green eyes glinting with something wild and untamed. "You look like someone who could use a little fun."

"Fun doesn't pay the bills," Ceige shoots back before she can stop herself—but even as she speaks, her pulse kicks up a notch, throbbing in her throat like the echo of distant hooves. It only gets worse when Sloane closes the remaining space between them with bold steps that feel less like walking and more like storming into battle.

"And I'm not interested in your games," Ceige adds—too quickly—her voice fumbling to regain footing on an already crumbling ledge.

Sloane tilts her head slightly to one side—a wolf sizing up its rival before going for the throat.

"Not even a little?" she murmurs again—soft this time but dangerous still—as though daring Ceige to flinch under the weight of their proximity now gone unbearably intimate.

Every inch of Sloane seems to vibrate with chaotic energy: magnetic yet destructive; alluring yet lethal; impossible not to notice yet equally impossible to fully grasp without getting scorched by it first-hand somehow.

"You know you're just as curious about me as I am about *you*," Sloane presses softly while still advancing one measured step after another toward where Ceige silently retreats backward inch by inch until finally.

"Curiosity killed the Judex," Ceige says. Her voice is steady. Almost. Beneath it, a tremor threatens to crack the surface. Their breaths mingle in the sharp air, a warmth rising between them that cuts through the cold like a blade.

"Then let's see how the Judex plays with fire." Sloane steps closer. One step, then another, slow and deliberate, until the desk stops Ceige's retreat. The edge bites into her butt. Nowhere left to go. No space left between them—just heat and the smell of something dangerous. Wood polish and smoke.

Sloane's breath ghosts over Ceige's cheek, warm against the chill that clings to the room like frost on glass. "Testing my resolve?" Ceige asks. One brow arches, her heart pounding a rhythm she can't control. She doesn't lean into Sloane's warmth—doesn't move at all—but every taut muscle in her body screams for release.

"No," Sloane whispers, her words soft as embers flickering low in the dark. "Testing what you really want."

The challenge ripples through the air between them. Each word sharp as a blade, cutting through Ceige's defenses. She doesn't answer—not yet—but she feels her armor shift, feels it fracture, piece by piece. Sloane moves closer still, heat radiating from her skin like wildfire searching for kindling. The ice around Ceige begins to crack.

"You're deluded," Ceige says at last, her voice flat but not steady enough to hide its wavering edges. "If you think you know what I want."

Sloane smiles—a flash of teeth that dances on the line between feral and mischievous—and for an instant, her eyes soften into something else entirely: open, vulnerable. Then it's gone again, swallowed by mischief wrapped in danger.

"Am I?" she asks. Her tone lilts upward, teasing but firm enough to linger. "What's life without risk? Or should I say—a lot of risk?"

"Life's about survival," Ceige counters quietly. The words fall heavy between them like stones dropped into still water. "Something you forget with your reckless abandon."

Sloane tilts her head just slightly—enough for her hair to catch the light as her grin tilts darker and sharper at its corners. "I'm still alive," she murmurs, leaning even closer now, so close their foreheads nearly touch. "While you're already dead inside."

The room shrinks around them until nothing remains but this—them—suspended in a haze too thick to breathe but too intoxicating to escape from.

Ceige swallows hard against the pull that wraps itself around her chest like barbed wire tightening inch by inch.

"Let's burn it all down."

And just like that—it ignites.

Ceige moves before thought can take hold: pivots sharply on her heel and twists Sloane with her—a blur of motion as cold metal presses against Sloane's spine instead of hers now.

The desk groans under their weight; papers flutter and fall like dying moths caught in sudden chaos—a storm they've conjured together without speaking a word.

Ceige doesn't let go.

Neither does Sloane.

Between them—it blazes still.

"Not so cocky now, are we?" Ceige growls. A smirk pulls at her lips as she watches Sloane's breath hitch, surprise flashing in those sharp green eyes. The thrill courses through her veins. The hunter has cornered her prey.

But then Sloane smiles—defiant, mocking. "You think this is control?" Her voice drips with challenge. "You've only made it interesting."

"Interesting." Ceige leans closer. Her words drop low, a private murmur meant for Sloane alone. "You don't even know the meaning."

The air between them tightens. Thickens. Outside, a storm gathers, but its fury pales next to the charge sparking in this room. Inches separate their faces now, the rest of the world dissolving into shadow and static.

It's just them.

Electricity crackles.

Danger trembles on their tongues.

"Kiss me," Sloane taunts. Her eyes gleam with mischief, but there's an edge beneath the bravado—fear running alongside desire like rival rivers threatening to overflow.

Ceige doesn't hesitate. She closes the space between them in a sudden crash—lips colliding, teeth clashing. It's not a kiss; it's a fight. A battle fought without weapons but leaving bruises all the same. She grips Sloane's jaw until flesh yields beneath her fingers, holding her steady—holding her here—as if she could trap the chaos spiraling around them.

"Goddamn," Sloane gasps against her mouth, fingers clawing into Ceige's cropped hair. Her nails bite at the scalp, sharp and unforgiving, sending a jolt straight down Ceige's spine. It stings sweetly—a reminder of how thin the line between pain and pleasure can be.

"God. Damn," Ceige rasps back. Her voice is rough, strained with something dangerous bubbling just beneath her skin. She pulls back an inch—just enough to meet Sloane's gaze head-on. And there it is: fire burning bright and wild in those green depths. It sparks something deep within Ceige—something raw and vulnerable that she doesn't dare name.

She stamps it out.

Focuses instead on the heat thrumming between them.

"Show me who you really are," Ceige breathes, her control fracturing as Sloane's proximity threatens everything she's built. The hunger in her voice betrays her—she's already falling.

Sloane's fingers ghost along her jaw. "You won't like what you find." Her touch is light but her eyes are predator-dark.

Their lips meet like a blade sliding home—precise, inevitable, fatal. They war for dominance, each kiss a battle neither can afford to lose. Their bodies entangle like weapons crossed, every point of contact both victory and surrender.

The room fades into motionless silence—only their breaths remain now: rapid, uneven gasps echoing off cluttered walls as hands press and pull, grasping for purchase in a war neither can afford to lose.

Each touch burns hotter than the last. Each gasp raises the stakes higher. Every moment teeters on collapse.

Sloane growls low in her throat as she yanks Ceige closer—her grip iron-tight on trembling arms marked by bruises yet to bloom. "Not running yet?" she warns through gritted teeth—a threat laced with something softer underneath: need.

"Shut up," Ceige snarls back—but inside she quakes with pleasure: exhilaration warring with dread, desire twisted up with doubt until they're indistinguishable from each other.

This chaos—it feels alive between them. A fleeting warmth amidst Eiskorps's endless cold. But warmth has its dangers.

Somewhere at the edges of her thoughts, regret stirs faintly—a whisper through static: *This will not last.* This cannot last without breaking everything they are... or everything they pretend to be.

The kisses deepen anyway. The gasps echo louder anyway. Two rivals locked tight in a web they spun themselves—a tangled snare made of lust and fury and ambition too sharp to ignore.

They cut like glass.

They seep through skin, bone, and resolve.

"You're not getting off that easy," Ceige murmurs, her voice low, rough—an edge honed sharp enough to cut. She leans in close, so close that her breath brushes Sloane's lips, melting the space between them for just a moment before the chill reclaims it.

Sloane smiles. No—smirks. That maddening spark dances in her green eyes like sunlight playing across ice. "Too bad," she purrs, every word dripping with insolence. "I like getting off easy." Her hands move slowly, teasingly, up Ceige's sides. Fingers glide over her jacket—not stripping it away but nudging it loose with deliberate languor. A test. A game. One they both know can't be won without cost.

Ceige doesn't flinch. Not yet. But her warning comes soft and sharp: "This the wrong thing in the wrong place at the wrong time."

"Right."

This is dangerous ground—they both feel it humming beneath their feet. Every touch commands more heat than either of them should dare in Eiskorps's icy grip. It sparks and smolders between them: raw friction born of fire meeting frost. Vulnerability? No—this game isn't for the weak or the willing to yield.

Sloane's touch shifts; fingers press boldly now, finding skin under layers meant to withstand this frozen world. She explores as if mapping unfamiliar territory, bold yet measured, seeking answers Ceige isn't ready to give. But Ceige moves too—her hands ghost over Sloane's frame with calculated precision, peeling away fabric with haunting patience. Worshipful? No—it's greed disguised as care.

Everything between them is electric—a current neither will admit surrenders control.

Ceige growls, voice rough as gravel under boots. Her hands trace downward, under and in—slowly at first—the movement intentional, ruthless in its deliberation. Her fingers find flesh and draw gasps from Sloane's lips—gasps that turn sharp-edged and breathless in the space of heartbeats.

Each sound is music; every reaction is battle won.

"God," Sloane breathes finally—a prayer or a curse or maybe both at once—"you're impossible." There's no venom behind it now; instead: something desperate and dangerously soft that cuts deeper than any blade could manage here where frost reigns supreme.

"You're one to talk," Ceige bites back through clenched teeth—the words steady even as chaos swirls deep beneath her surface calm like an avalanche threatening to break loose forever against the industrial unbroken silence.

"Let me show you how it's done," Sloane says, her voice low, a blade hidden in silk.

Before Ceige can respond, Sloane shifts. Hands, hips, leverage—she twists their positions with fluid precision. The desk groans beneath the force. The air snaps taut, charged, like the instant before lightning splits the sky. Ceige feels the jolt, adrenaline biting at her veins, instinct rearing up—a primal demand: fight or flight.

"Oh, bold," Ceige breathes through clenched teeth, her lips curling into something between a grin and a snarl. "Let's see it then."

"You'll regret that challenge." The words spill from Sloane's lips like smoke curling through cold air—sultry, dangerous, intoxicating. A wicked smile flickers there too, sharp enough to slice resolve clean in half. Ceige doesn't need to hear more; she already feels it sinking its claws into her—a fiery pull that blurs edges and reason.

Their bodies clash and tumble in tangled rhythm—push meets pull meets resistance—and yet the weight between them is heavier than mere flesh and bone. It carries stories untold but not forgotten, ambitions worn as armor and wounds bleeding beneath careful seams.

This is not just want.

This is war.

Sloane moves like water over stone—fluid hands finding purchase on Ceige's body with unnerving precision. Every touch is deliberate, each stroke a subtle strike meant to disarm. She knows where to press; she always knows where to press. Fingers trace hipbone, linger just long enough to ignite sparks before diving in—cutting through shields like flame across dry earth.

Ceige gasps—the sound betraying her before she can catch it—and with that single slip, her facade cracks wide open. For an instant, everything hangs there: raw and exposed in the flickering dark between them.

"This is war," Ceige thinks. And they both know it.

Sloane breathes heavily now—her sound low and dangerous as it spills over parted lips—and retaliates with touches that are equal parts torment and temptation. Each movement is surgical precision wrapped in chaos—careful strokes crafted to burn.

But Ceige finds her footing again. She forces herself steady despite the heat twisting through her core like molten iron poured into fragile glass. With a hard pivot she reclaims ground—grabs hold of Sloane and slams them both back into the desk once more. The collision of their bodies ripples outward—their limbs tangling violently as dominance shifts again.

Sloane grins in response—a flash of teeth illuminated by wicked intent—and pushes harder with hands that map their way through Ceige's pleasure as if staking claim over uncharted territory. Predator's hands, calculating even amid frenzy—the kind that mark not for possession but for victory.

Ceige begins to quake.

"Careful," Sloane murmurs, her words dripping venom laced with honey. "You're making this too easy."

Her laughter follows—a low growl from deep within her chest—and it sends shivers racing down Ceige's spine despite herself.

Ceige leans forward into the heat of it—a collision of willpower meeting desire—but refuses to cede ground entirely. She arches into Sloane's touch even as irritation boils underneath every pulse thrumming through her veins like warning drums.

"Easy?" she hisses now between clenched teeth—a challenge sharpened by sarcasm yet tinged faintly with anticipation she won't name aloud. "You haven't even s-scored yet."

"Let's raise the stakes then," Sloane whispers now against her ear—a blade turned edgewise against vulnerability itself—as she pulls Ceige closer still until there's no space left untouched by tension sparking between their bodies like live wires crossing paths midstorm. "Unless you're scared."

But Sloane's push is relentless. Gentle, then not. A game she plays so well it feels more like instinct than strategy. Fingers trace paths that blur lines—domination and submission twisting together until Ceige can't untangle which is which anymore. She teeters, the edge giving way beneath her feet.

"I want to see you break." Sloane's voice is low, smug, soft enough to feel intimate but sharp enough to cut. Her eyes catch the light, gleaming like embers in the dark.

That spark ignites something hot and dangerous inside Ceige—a fire fighting against the ice threatening to consume them both. No thought now, only retaliation. Her hands move on their own, seeking weaknesses with ruthless precision, every shiver and stifled breath from Sloane feeding the inferno.

The moments collide into one another—raw, electric, endless. Urgency crackles in the air between them as hunger devours hesitation. The office around them dissolves into insignificance; shadows lurch and shift under cold fluorescent lights that buzz faintly above them. Within the icy fortress of Eiskorps, they create something warmer than it has ever known before. It blazes hotter than either of them expects.

It builds like an inferno—ravenous and all-consuming—until they are engulfed together in the blaze.

Release crashes through them with bitten lips and muffled cries, bodies trembling in the searing glow, consumed by the flames they've sparked. They are caught as though trapped in the heart of a conflagration too fierce to endure, its combustion consuming everything else: betrayal, rivalry, history—all incinerated and left as smoke in its wake. For one breathless moment, there is only this.

"Fuck," Ceige murmurs into the heavy silence that follows. A whisper filled with exhaustion and something else she refuses to name. Her chest rises and falls as realization seeps in like cold through a cracked windowpane: they've crossed some unspoken line yet again. Exposed too much of themselves on the ice-slick battlefield where secrets are currency and vulnerability is fatal.

The warmth between them flickers but does not die—not yet—and that frightens Ceige more than anything else.

Sloane shifts first—always first—masking whatever lies beneath with bravado polished just enough to glint in the light like steel. "Keep your guard up, Ceige," she says softly, her voice thick with something unsteady but quickly buried. "You never know when the next shot will come."

The words settle between them like frost—sharp-edged and cold—and just like that, reality creeps back in. The ghosts of desire retreat into Eiskorps's biting chill as rules reassert themselves, each one falling into place with cruel precision.

Ceige nods once, refusing to let her expression betray her racing thoughts or pounding heart. No space for weakness now—not here where it could cost them more than either can afford to lose.

This isn't just another mission anymore; it's something else entirely—something tangled and dangerous that neither dares acknowledge aloud but both feel pressing against their chests with every breath.

Sloane holds her gaze for a heartbeat before letting go—a quiet retreat masked as indifference—but Ceige feels it anyway: the same tension she fights clawing at Sloane too.

Then it breaks.

Ceige steps back slowly—deliberately—as though moving too quickly might shatter whatever fragile truce lingers in their wake. The heat remains behind like a ghost pressed against her skin; no amount of distance erases it completely.

She smooths her rumpled clothes with trembling hands made clumsy by adrenaline still burning through her veins. Around them Eiskorps presses in again—the office cold and unyielding once more—but for Ceige nothing feels quite steady anymore.

Why does she always get under my skin?

The thought slips through before she can crush it down where it belongs—buried deep alongside every other question Sloane has carved into her soul when Ceige wasn't paying attention or was too foolish to care.

Her fingers still briefly on a wrinkle she cannot smooth out...then release altogether, as if surrendering at last to what cannot be fixed.

Straightening her spine despite muscles that threaten rebellion at every rigid movement, Ceige steps away again—further this time—but she does not look back at Sloane until she knows her armor is firmly restored.

"Well, that was... something."

Her voice is steady. Too steady. Inside, waves crash against the fragile cliffs of her resolve. The walls she built—brick by painstaking brick—are falling, crumbled pieces scattering around her feet. Zero fucks given—wasn't that the rule? Her own scoff cuts like a blade. She needs to lock it down, seal it tight. Emotions have no place here. Not in this frozen wasteland.

Sloane leans back against the desk's edge, her breath ragged as if she's surfaced from deep water, barely alive. Her wild hair, streaked with sweat, encircles her face like a crown of chaos. Those vivid green eyes pierce Ceige, sharp and unrelenting—a storm behind them, mischief swirling at the edges but something darker twisting beneath. "Next time," she says, her lips quirking into a smirk that doesn't quite hold, "try not to pant like a dog in heat." The bravado is thin—cracked ice stretched over unknown depths—but she throws it out there anyway, sharp as a knife.

"Right." Ceige crosses her arms, grounding herself against the pull Sloane has always had on her, steadying when everything feels off-balance. "Because you were so composed." The words come quick, instinctive—a jab meant to keep them in their rhythm. That dance they do: sparring even when everything else feels like it's falling apart. But this time, something has shifted. A crack has opened between them, and Ceige feels its pull like gravity.

"All jokes aside," Sloane says suddenly, tilting her head just enough for the teasing glint to drain from her eyes. What replaces it is sharper, heavier—a blade unsheathed. "You know I have my own reasons for going after Eira."

The air thickens between them, heavy and cold like the moments before a storm breaks open the sky. Ceige feels it settle in her chest like a weight pulling her heart downward. Sloane isn't just playing games anymore; this is deeper than tactics or strategy—it's personal. It always is with her. "What do you mean?" Ceige asks because she has to.

Sloane pushes off the desk with languid grace, stepping forward until there's no more space between them. Her presence wraps around Ceige again—dangerous and magnetic all at once. "Let's just say I've got a vested interest in that woman." Her words drip with venom laced in charm, delivered with an undertone that promises destruction masked in beauty. "Eira's been playing god with lives... mine included."

Ceige narrows her eyes at the admission—sharp now, defensive—the instinct to shield herself rising like armor from within. "And you?" The question slips out before she can stop it; she hates how small it sounds in the space between them but asks anyway because she has to know where she stands now that the game board feels stacked against her. "Am I just your pawn?"

Sloane shrugs one shoulder with that infuriating poise of hers—graceful as a dancer who knows every step before it's taken—calm even while chaos rages around them both. "Isn't that what we both are?" Her voice lilts upward slightly—not quite mocking but close enough to sting—as if survival itself were some twisted game they're only pretending not to enjoy playing. "Two players stuck on opposite sides of someone else's sick chessboard?" She tilts closer again; her dark laugh is soft but razor-sharp when it comes out: "I mean... come on—it's not like you showed up here expecting tea and crumpets."

"Maybe I was hoping for less mayhem," Ceige fires back immediately—defensive now—but the bite in her voice doesn't mask what sits between them: truth laid bare like an open wound neither will admit to seeing.

The fire in Sloane's eyes burns hot. Fierce. Unapologetic.

"Eira's got secrets," she says, her voice softer now, almost vulnerable. But not quite. "Secrets that could destroy everything Eiskorps stands for. I want to expose her. And then I want to kill her." She pauses, letting the words settle like ash after an explosion. "Revenge," she adds, her tone sharpening like a blade, "for what she did to my sister."

Revenge. The word finds its mark and lodges itself deep in Ceige's chest. Something shifts—a piece of the puzzle sliding into place with a sharp click.

"So it's personal," Ceige says quietly, her words cutting through the space between them.

"It always has been." Sloane doesn't flinch. There's steel there—unbending, unyielding. "But I can't do this alone." She hesitates, just for a fraction of a second, before driving the knife in deeper: "And neither can you."

A laugh escapes Ceige's lips, sharp and humorless. "Teaming up with my rival Judex?" Her voice is brittle, as though trying to lighten the weight pressing on both their shoulders but failing miserably. "Sounds like a death wish."

She watches Sloane smile—a quick flash of teeth, more wolf than woman—and something heavier flickers behind it, dark and unspoken. They both know the risks. They always know the risks. Betrayal lies coiled between them like a snake waiting to strike.

"Trust me," Sloane says simply. Her words slide into the air like smoke—intangible yet suffocating. "We can take her down together... You and I? We make one hell of a team."

Trust me.

The phrase lingers, heavy as stone dropping into deep water. Ceige feels it pull at her—an anchor or maybe an invitation into something far more dangerous than betrayal.

"Yeah," she says finally, shaking her head as if to clear it. "Good luck with that."

Her fingers twitch at her sides, itching for the cold reassurance of steel—a weapon that doesn't whisper promises it won't keep. They're Judex first and lovers second; Ceige reminds herself of this fact with every beat of her heart.

"Just think about it," Sloane replies, stepping back into shadow but leaving the challenge hanging in the air between them like freezing mist after a storm. Her gaze sharpens as she adds: "But remember—you're not just hunting Eira anymore; you're hunting truth now too. And truths? They'll cut deeper than any blade."

"Hunting's what I do," Ceige shoots back automatically, the defiance in her voice masking what simmers underneath—uncertainty wrapped in layers of cold resolve.

Sloane pivots toward the door without another word; her movements are smooth, feline—a predator retreating but not conceding ground. The blizzard outside howls against the building like some feral beast kept at bay by thin walls and thinner convictions.

"Stay sharp," Ceige calls after her as Sloane's silhouette threatens to dissolve into shadow. For one fragile moment—one crack in the armor—Ceige allows herself to imagine they might actually pull this off together.

Then reality crashes back over her like the storm outside.

Movement in the doorway.

Sloane is waiting.

"What's it gonna be, Ceige?" The question comes from across the room—not loud but cutting all the same.

Sloane's voice dances through the cluttered office like electricity sparking off frayed wires—dangerous and impossible to ignore.

Ceige doesn't answer right away; instead, she watches Sloane standing there framed by scattered papers and flickering lightbulbs overhead—the wild tangle of curls catching fractured light until they gleam like some cracked halo above her head.

Chaotic, electric energy surrounds Sloane like armor—or maybe camouflage—and Ceige feels its pull even now... especially now.

"Well?" The teasing twist in Sloane's mouth is sharper than ever—a smile made for breaking hearts or splitting skulls depending on which side of it you land on.

Ceige exhales slowly through gritted teeth.

"We getting on with this or what? You going to keep brooding?"

Brooding? No, that's not it. Ceige sits in the stillness, her voice calm but razor-edged. "Maybe I'm just contemplating the wreckage you leave behind." She doesn't let herself glance at Sloane, doesn't let those green eyes—sharp as broken glass—see how much the sex nearly shattered her. Because this is a knife's-edge game they're playing. One step wrong, and it's death for them both.

Sloane steps closer, a predator weaving through shadows, her grin curling like smoke. "Wreckage is my specialty," she says, her voice light, playful—but there's steel beneath it. The distance between them shrinks, air tightening like a noose. Ceige feels the pull again: raw and feral, something buried deep clawing to get out. She clenches her jaw and forces the rush of heat back into cold control.

"You know what they say about business and pleasure?" Sloane murmurs, close enough now that Ceige can feel the faint warmth radiating from her skin. "Dangerous combination." A pause, deliberate. "But thrilling."

"Thrilling isn't the word I'd use." Ceige lets the words lay like stones into the heavy silence between them. Her fingers twitch toward the grip of her gun—not a threat. Not yet. But an anchor, steady and cool against her palm. This is a dance on thin ice, and one misstep plunges them both into chaos.

Sloane tilts her head, curiosity glinting in those damn emerald eyes. "Face it, Ceige—you're intrigued." Her voice lowers, coiling tighter around Ceige's resolve like barbed wire. "You want to know why. Why the hit? Why I care about Eira so much? Why I'll chase her to the ends of Cryosium?" Her lips twist into something sly, dangerous. "And maybe you're wondering why I'm here with *you*."

Ceige exhales sharply through her nose like a bull seeing red but refusing to charge—yet. "Curiosity killed the cat," she says coldly, fighting to keep the tremor out of her voice and heat off her cheeks. She straightens her spine like that will fortify what's left of her defenses before adding: "And it won't save yours if you don't start making sense."

Sloane laughs softly under her breath—not mockery but something dangerously close to amusement—and takes another step forward, breaking boundaries Ceige didn't realize she had reconstructed. "Ah," Sloane purrs, "but you're no ordinary cat." Her gaze brushes over Ceige like a blade testing soft flesh for weakness. "You're too careful for that—safe behind walls built high as mountains." Another beat; then softer still: "But even mountains crumble."

The warning catches in Ceige's throat before it makes it out—icy and edged as a blade slipped between ribs: "Keep your distance, Vale." Her tone is frostbite cold now; nothing soft has survived in Cryosium except what hides deep down—and this woman knows too well where to dig.

"Distance," Sloane echoes with a smirk painted on her lips like war paint—challenging yet maddeningly calm all at once. She leans back slightly, as if considering it, but doesn't retreat far. The room chills around them despite their shared warmth; maybe that's what happens when two forces stretch tension taut enough to break glass—or bone—or both.

"How's that working for you?" Sloane asks finally, tilting her head again but without venom this time—no mockery either...just truth pried bare like an exposed wound. "Bet loneliness suits you better than trust does."

"Better than trusting a rival Judex."

Sharper than she wanted, but no less true. Trust isn't something Ceige has to give—not here, not in Cryosium. Trust is a cracked blade that turns in your hand.

"Maybe it's time you stopped seeing shadows in every corner." Sloane edges closer, her breath brushing Ceige's cheek, warm enough to melt the room's chill for half a second. "You think I'm reckless? You think I don't have my reasons? I do, Ceige. Real ones."

"Your reasons mean nothing to me." Ceige fights to keep her voice steady, even as her resolve trembles like glass on the verge of breaking. Desire flickers—a dangerous flame—but the ice is thicker, stronger. "The bounty matters. Therefore, Eira matters."

"The contract." Sloane steps back, her face hardening as if she's slipped on armor. The shift cuts like a broken promise; whatever invisible thread pulled them close frays now, snapping apart—thin ice cracking beneath weighted steps. "But what if I told you there's more than that? What if I told you I know things—things that could rip all this apart?"

"Then say it." Ceige feels the words claw their way free, raw and jagged. Her control slips as frustration surges hot under her skin. Still, somewhere beneath the heat, something colder stirs—curiosity gnawing with sharp little teeth.

"Later." Sloane pauses long enough for the silence to sharpen its edge, then lets the word drop like a stone into still water. "Right now, you need to know this isn't just business for me." Her eyes burn with something fierce and unguarded—a signal flare behind the cracks in her composure. "I'm risking everything for this, Ceige. This isn't about Eira, not really—not anymore. It's about my sister. And finding out what really happened to her."

The words hang heavy between them, sticky with implication. Sloane's voice softens but doesn't lose its weight as she adds, "Our paths are connected, whether you want them to be or not."

"Connected?" The word spits out bitter and sharp as bile on Ceige's tongue. She shakes her head once—short, violent—then again for good measure; anger flares quick and hot enough to burn through doubt. "You want me tangled up in your revenge? That's suicide."

"Or it's survival," Sloane counters smoothly, without missing a beat. The heat behind her falters only briefly before cooling into something harder, sharper—a challenge reshaped into steel resolve. "This is bigger than both of us—don't you see that? But it won't wait forever."

Ceige exhales slowly through gritted teeth, letting silence answer first because her words might break something irrevocable if they come too soon. When they do come, they're cold as Cryosium's winds and twice as unforgiving: "I'm out."

The words hang in the air like a cocked hammer.

But Sloane doesn't wait for it to fall. She's already moving, a sharp pivot on her heel, slicing through the tension as she strides for the door.

"Wait!" Ceige lunges forward, but it's instinct, not strategy—the kind of reflex you regret even as you act. Her fingers snag nothing but empty air. Sloane slips through the doorway like smoke on the wind, leaving behind only the faint scent of leather and gunmetal.

Ceige freezes in the wake of her retreat. The door clicks shut with the finality of a guillotine. The room, once alive with heat and venom, is now only shadows and silence.

And yet Sloane lingers.

Not her body, but her last glance. That look—half defiance, half something softer—clings to Ceige like frostbite under her skin, refusing to let go.

The storm outside screams against the windowpanes. Inside, another storm churns—in Ceige's gut, her chest, her head. Questions roll in like thunderclouds: What fuels Sloane's fire? How deep does her vendetta run? And why can't Ceige stop chasing shadows she'll never catch?

"Fuck." The word hisses out between clenched teeth as Ceige paces tight circles what feels like a circus ring. Her boots scuff against scattered papers and toppled chairs. She drags a hand through her messy hair like she's trying to rip out the frustration boiling inside her.

Too many threads. Too many knots pulling tighter by the second.

She tries to clear her head—focus—but it keeps coming back to this: Sloane complicates everything. Every crossed path, every stolen glance is a snare waiting to tighten around Ceige's throat.

She grits her teeth hard enough to hurt and forces herself out of her head—out of this room suffocating with ghosts of what was just done and what wasn't.

Focus on *Eira Halstead.* Not Sloane—not those wild green eyes or that smirk carved from stone—and certainly not whatever divine poison lingers between them. Eira Halstead is the mission—a bounty that could mean survival in a world clawing to swallow Ceige whole.

So why does it feel like every step forward just pulls her deeper into quicksand?

Ceige takes a breath and shoves open the door, mindlessly slips through hallways and finds her way out. The blizzard outside punches her square in the face—cold so sharp it feels alive, biting down into exposed skin like teeth gnashing bone.

Good. She needs that bite to pull herself out of the mire of thought and memory.

The street sprawls before her—a white wasteland stripped bare by ice and wind. Broken shadows flicker across gray walls like ghosts trying to come back to life. Snowflakes swirl in tight circles around piles of frozen debris, looking delicate until they cut across your face sharp as glass.

Each step crunches beneath Ceige's boots, every sound amplified by the eerie quiet of Cryosium's streets at night. Desolation hums here—not loud but steady—like blood dripping into still water.

The scars on this city are everywhere—the same as hers: deep, jagged wounds that don't heal so much as calcify into armor.

Her breaths puff out in clouds that vanish too quickly against the cold air; she imagines they're fragments of herself flung into oblivion one exhale at a time.

"Focus," she mutters again under her breath—audible only to herself, lost before it hits anything real.

But focus doesn't come easy when visions of Sloane still blaze beneath closed eyelids—or even open ones because those eyes are burned there now: green fire glowing through sheets of white snow.

A rival. A Judex. A lover. A wild card pulling strings Ceige didn't even know existed until now.

And something else entirely—something Ceige doesn't want to name but can already feel coiling tight inside her chest like a snake readying to strike or embrace—it doesn't matter which because either way it will kill you eventually.

Her fist tightens around nothing but air.

She keeps walking anyway.

Snow falls heavy. Too heavy.

Ceige pulls the collar of her coat tighter around her neck, the coarse fabric biting into her skin. The cold gnaws at her like a feral thing, but it's the thoughts she can't shake that chill her deeper.

The bounty hangs in front of her, a ghost she can't touch—Eira Halstead. Blood-streaked promises and secrets buried beneath frost. This isn't just another job; it's a thread tied to something larger, something she almost doesn't want to unravel. Almost.

She turns a corner and nearly trips over a rusted trash bin, spilling its guts onto the street—bones picked clean, wrappers slick with grease. She steps wide of it, muttering under her breath. Cryosium doesn't care for neatness, or dignity. It eats everything you are, leaves you hollow, cold.

Her boots crunch over snow and filth as she scans the alleys. The city stretches before her in jagged angles of pale light and endless shadow. Every corner hides teeth; every shadow breathes lies. Trust here is rarer than warmth, more fragile than ice on a thawing river.

And then there's Sloane.

Ceige shakes her head, hard, shoving the thought aside like a blade from an old wound. But it festers anyway. What drives Sloane? Not survival—no, not just that. Something darker, sharper. Revenge? Justice? Or is it all some sick game where neither of them ever wins?

She rounds another corner and sees movement—a flicker low in an alleyway half-swallowed by drifts of snow and blackened refuse. Her hand moves without thought, finding the hilt of her blade beneath her coat as she edges closer to the darkened doorway.

Rats scatter across rotted crates, their tails vanishing into shadow.

"Fuck," she mutters under her breath and steps back onto the main street. The tension in her chest doesn't ease; it tightens instead, coiling like wire pulled too taut.

Sloane presses into her thoughts again. That wild hair damp with sweat and melted frost. That smirk—defiance turned razor sharp against the night sky. The way they collided was fire meeting fire, two predators circling but neither willing to yield ground.

The memory lingers too long—long enough to burn—and Ceige curses herself for letting it creep back in again.

"Don't," she growls at no one but herself.

But Sloane has already infected something deeper in her mind—a dangerous whisper that maybe this isn't just hatred or vengeance or survival anymore. Maybe Sloane has become more than an obstacle; maybe she's part of some answer Ceige doesn't even know she's looking for.

She exhales slowly through gritted teeth and keeps moving forward as ice crystals swirl in torn gusts around her boots.

"Goddamnit," she breathes low and bitterly into the cold air that refuses to stop cutting at her skin. This place—it doesn't stop for anyone not willing to bite back harder than it claws at you.

Chapter 3

The tunnels breathe.

Cold, metallic air.

Ceige moves like a shadow, each step a whisper on the frozen concrete. The pipes above drip with ice, their bitter tang curling into her lungs, cutting each inhale to ribbons. Glass shards in her chest. The darkness clings to her like an old lover—familiar, unyielding, full of quiet promises and threats. She belongs here. She hunts here.

A faint scuff stops her mid-step.

Her pulse tightens. Her fingers flex for the blade hidden against her hip. From the gloom, a figure peels itself free—Sloane Vale, sharp angles and wild hair, hungry eyes glinting like broken gemstones under frost. Ceige's stomach twists against her will.

"What are you doing here?" she spits. Her breath puffs white in the icy air, words carrying blades.

"Charming as ever, Rivers." Sloane leans back against the frost-rimed wall, all casual defiance. But Ceige sees it—the coil of tension beneath that smirk, the way her shoulders don't quite relax. "Figured I'd find you playing hide-and-seek with your trauma somewhere grimier."

"Cut it out." Ceige's voice is low, tight, sharp enough to cleave through the brittle cold between them. Her hand brushes the hilt of her knife—muscle memory—and she narrows her gaze. "What do you know about Eira?"

"More than I want to," Sloane snaps back, the fire in her tone melting some of the ice in the air. She shifts away from the wall, eyes flickering with something dangerous. "Biotech horrors. Vanishing acts. Corporate ghosts clawing at the edges of decency." A beat passes; her gaze drills into Ceige's like a blade testing armor. "I'm not just poking around in this mess—I'm digging graves."

"For who?" Ceige keeps her voice steady, though she feels it—heaviness curling tight in her gut. She is starting to wonder if her name is on the list.

Sloane's mouth hardens into a flat line before she speaks again. "Enemies."

The word lands heavy between them.

"My sister," Sloane says quietly now, venom bleeding out into raw edges. "She didn't make it out of one of their labs." Her jaw tightens as if holding back more words—or pain—and for just a flicker of a moment, Ceige sees something fragile there, something bruised. Then it's gone.

"You said that before, but I still don't understand," Ceige exhales slowly against the cold as memories scrape through her mind like nails against stone. The last time they met... passion and pain between them like an open wound still weeping red. "And I still don't trust you. So why shouldn't I slit your throat right now?" she asks evenly.

"You could try." There's that smirk again—but it falters at the edges this time as Sloane takes a step closer and lowers her voice to match Ceige's razor-sharp tone: "Or you could focus on Eira before they swallow us all whole."

Silence rolls in heavily around them.

"Trust isn't free," Ceige mutters finally.

"Nothing is." Sloane shrugs but doesn't retreat—her head tilts slightly as though daring Ceige to push harder or walk away entirely.

Ceige studies her for a long moment—green eyes lit by defiance meeting hers without flinching—and then nods once: reluctant agreement carved into stone.

"Talk."

"Rumors of experiments on people. Taking them apart and trying to rebuild them. Frankenstein level shit," Sloane says quickly now—as if relieved Ceige hasn't left yet but also knowing time hangs thin around them like frayed wire ready to snap apart at any second.

Her words tumble faster, eyes fever-bright in the dim light. "People go missing from the Frost District. Not the ones anyone misses—at first. Then it spread. Higher. Riskier targets. Some come back... wrong. Walking but not alive. Others?" She shakes her head. "Just pieces left. Like someone's testing how far they can push the human body before it breaks."

Ceige's jaw tightens. She's heard whispers in the Underground—talk of screams echoing from sealed labs, of bodies moving with mechanical imprecision through shadowed streets, of eyes that reflect light like mirrors.

"The missing ones that return," Sloane continues, voice dropping lower, "they're stronger. Faster. But there's nothing left inside. No memories, no will. Perfect soldiers, right? Except the changes don't hold. They... deteriorate. Messily." Her fingers drum against her thigh, a nervous tell. "Found one of Eira's early subjects. What was left of her. The modifications were eating her from inside out, turning tissue to something else. Something that shouldn't exist."

"How deep does this go?" Ceige asks, though she suspects she already knows.

"City's elite are funding it. Military's interested. And Eira?" Sloane's laugh is bitter as winter wind. "She's just getting started. Each failure pushes her to try something worse. More invasive. More ambitious. She thinks she can perfect it, control it. But you can't control something this wrong without becoming a monster yourself."

A distant scream echoes through the tunnels—might be human, might be something else. Both women instinctively tense, hands moving to weapons. The sound fades, but the unease lingers like frost on skin.

"My sister," Sloane adds quietly, "she was one of the first. Volunteered for what she thought was routine medical testing. By the time I tracked her down..." She stops, swallows hard. "There wasn't enough left to bury."

Finally: "We need to move."

Ceige doesn't hesitate this time—just nods again brusquely before following close behind when Sloane takes off down another stretch of darkness where flickering lights barely cling onto life above their heads anymore.

Ceige steps into the underground market.

Heat and smoke claw at her throat. The air is thick, clotted with sweat and something metallic—a tang that curls her stomach. Bodies press and sway, moving in a frantic rhythm of barter and survival. Shadows twist across grimy walls, faint light struggling to break through. Above it all, Cryosium looms, invisible but cold, its grip ever-present.

She scans the chaos. Faces blur together—a smear of desperation and deceit—but her senses are sharp, honed. Danger hums in her blood like a second pulse.

Ceige moves through the Underground market with practiced indifference, each step calculated to draw minimal attention. The cramped space buzzes with desperate energy—merchants hawking salvaged tech, medicine dealers promising miracle cures, the desperate seeking warmth or answers or both.

"Heard anything about Eiskorps?" she asks a scarred vendor, sliding him extra credits for his black-market stims. Her tone is casual, practiced—just another customer making conversation.

He stiffens slightly. "Don't mess with corp business, friend. Bad for health." His eyes dart left, though, toward a cluster of people huddled near a steam vent. Ceige notes the direction without obvious interest.

Across the market, Sloane's more direct approach creates ripples. She's cornered a man in a threadbare coat, his hands shaking as he clutches a bottle. "I used to clean there," he stammers when she presses. "Got out fast as I could. Some things you can't unsee—" He stumbles away before finishing, disappearing into the crowd.

A woman overhears Ceige asking about Eiskorps job openings. "Stay away from that place," she hisses, grabbing Ceige's arm. "My cousin took a night shift position three weeks ago. Haven't seen her since. They said she quit, but her credits are still in her account, untouched." xxx

Near the synthetic coffee stand, wild theories fly when Ceige simply says 'Eiskorp'. "They're breeding monsters in the sub-basements," one man insists, eyes glazed from cheap stims. "Saw something climb out of a vent once—had too many limbs, all wrong angles. And mirrors for eyes."

"That's nothing," another chimes in. "My brother's friend swears they're aliens—the blue ones not the grey ones—and they're trying to take over by wiping us humans right off the earth."

Ceige mentally files away the fragments of truth buried under hysteria. When she asks about the basement labs, the coffee vendor just shakes his head. "Look, you didn't hear this from me, but there's a reason they tripled the night guard rotation. Something down there needs containing."

"How do you know that, friend?"

Her 'friend' shrugs. "Triple coffee orders."

Sloane appears at Ceige's shoulder, her presence electric with barely contained energy. "They're all terrified," she mutters, low enough that only Ceige can hear. "But no one's got the full picture. Just pieces."

"Half the stories sound insane," Ceige responds quietly.

"Yeah, but which half?"

Before they can discuss further, the crowd parts slightly, and they hear it:

"Eira's experiments—" A man's voice, low and urgent, snakes through the noise. His hood hides his face, but his words sink like hooks into Ceige's chest. "They're using them on us!" Near him, a woman clutches a crumpled flyer marked with Eira Halstead's logo. Her hands tremble as if holding onto more than paper.

Ceige exhales sharply. "Using them on us? Huh."

Conspiratorially vague.

The hooded man turns toward a small gathering, his voice dropping lower. "My wife worked security. Upper levels. Safe, they said. Then they transferred her to basement detail." His fingers work nervously at his sleeve. "She came home... different. Stronger. Faster. Thought it was just stims at first. The extra money was good so I didn't ask much. Then—" He pulls back his sleeve, revealing a mass of bruises. "She didn't know her own strength anymore. Started forgetting things. People. Me."

"Where is she now?" someone asks.

"They took her back. Said she needed 'adjustment.'" His laugh is hollow. "That was two weeks ago. She sent a message saying she's okay, but I don't know. Now they're offering me a job. Same department. Say they need people with 'experience handling enhanced individuals.'"

The crowd shifts uncomfortably. A few edge away, but others lean in, hungry for more. Ceige catches Sloane's eye—this is more than random Underground paranoia. This is coordinated fear.

"Show them," the woman with the flyer urges. The man hesitates, then reaches into his coat for his pubcom. Security footage, grainy but clear enough: figures moving with inhuman speed through Eiskorps corridors, others with limbs bent at impossible angles, and one—Ceige's breath catches—with eyes that reflect light like mirrors, just like in the rumors.

"Could be fake," Ceige says, challenging the man.

"Enough," a new voice cuts through the murmurs. A government health enforcer, flanked by two others, their uniforms unmarked but their purpose clear. "This area is now closed for inspection. Clear out."

The crowd scatters like mercury, leaving Ceige and Sloane pressed against the shadows. The hooded man disappears, but not before dropping something—a keycard, its Eiskorps logo partially scratched off.

Sloane moves to grab it, but Ceige catches her wrist. The enforcers are still watching. Still waiting.

"Later," Ceige breathes. "They haven't noticed it yet."

"Yeah," Sloane's voice is tight with rage and promise. "Later."

They slip away as the enforcers begin their sweep, but Ceige can't shake the image of those mirrored eyes. She's seen her share of atrocities, but this...this is different. This is evolution forced at gunpoint, and Eira Halstead is holding the gun.

They slip into another section—free of enforcers—between clusters of dealers hunched over makeshift tables littered with black-market tech—scrap from another world—and sidestep their hungry eyes. The market seethes with tension; every glance feels like a weapon aimed at her back. Every step could lead to an ambush.

Then she spots him.

Silver goggles catch the dim light—a rival Judex leaning against a crumbling wall on the far side of the market. Too still. Too confident. Like he owns the air around him.

A smirk curves his mouth as his gaze locks onto hers.

Ceige doesn't flinch.

"Well, if it isn't the Ice Queen," he calls out, his voice slick with mockery that cuts through the din like glass scraping stone.

The crowd churns between them, unseeing, uncaring. Ceige's muscles tense as she gauges him—posture loose but coiled underneath, distance closing fast in her mind's eye.

"Don't you have someone else to bother?" Her reply slices back cold and sharp, each word deliberate.

"Everyone knows you took the Eira job. Even Eira. Uno reverse, bitch," he says. The smirk on his face widens just slightly.

Chaos explodes.

A crash, a scream.

The underground market shatters into motion, a hive turned frantic. Ceige feels it before she sees it—a ripple in the air, bodies colliding in a wave of fear and fury. The noise slashes through her focus, jagged and raw. She doesn't think. Thinking takes too long. She moves.

Through the crush of bodies, her heart slamming like a fist inside her chest, Ceige weaves—swift, sharp, deliberate. The air thickens with the metallic tang of adrenaline, panic hammering against her skull.

"Get down!" someone yells. She doesn't need to be told twice. Ceige drops low as a projectile tears past overhead, splinters flying like shrapnel as it obliterates a stall behind her. Shards of glass rain down, catching the dim light like fractured stars before they crash to the concrete with all the finality of gunfire.

She's already moving again. Zipps fly in, spreading trails of thick smoke designed to make it so hard to breathe you collapse to the ground.

Her boots drive forward, faster now, each step carving a path through the pandemonium. Ahead, Sloane's hair blazes like fire in the dark—a flicker of recognition in a sea of unfamiliar faces. She's shouting orders to traders clawing for an escape route, her voice breaking against the noise of collapsing stalls and pounding feet.

"Stick close!" Sloane hollers through the din.

"Joined at the hip!" Ceige snaps back, sarcasm sharp enough to cut through steel. But there's something else beneath it—something softer and unspoken that tugs at her chest before she shoves it aside. No time for that now.

Bodies slam into her from every angle, chaos spilling like blood from an open wound. Her gun is solid in her grip—a lifeline she won't let go of. The storm around them rages on as the man with silver goggles fires indiscriminately, but Ceige keeps moving forward because that's all she knows how to do: follow Sloane.

She bursts free from the market's prison with its smoke and sweat still clinging to her skin.

Cold air punches her lungs as she emerges into the open streets above—a battlefield no less dangerous than the hell below. The underground roar fades behind her only to be replaced by something sharper: gunfire cracking like snapping bones in the distance; boots striking ice-slick pavement; fear breathing heavy down her neck.

The health enforcers are shooting, but no one is sure what they are shooting at.

The wind greets her with a bite—an unbroken beast clawing at exposed skin and finding purchase even through layers of fabric. Frosted walls shimmer faintly under dim light as Ceige bolts through narrow streets carved from ice and shadow.

"Catch you later!" Sloane's taunt floats through the noise, sticky with derision that clings like tar. She smiles—a smile sharpened into something feral—and lets out a laugh that cuts through the dark like glass slicing flesh.

Gone.

Ceige moves. Each step on slick ground is measured risk made instinct—her boots finding fleeting purchase on streets edged with treachery but steeped in familiarity: **her territory**.

The wind snaps hard enough to sting but she welcomes its ferocity—it reminds her she's alive. Ice needles whip across raw skin; cold burns clean through layers until only survival remains.

Here there are no faces pressed tight into hers or hands grasping at escape routes—but there's no warmth either to mask intentions or soften edges.

Out here? Out here is truth. Out here is where Ceige thrives.

"Prudence isn't courage. It's knowing when to leave the chaos behind."

She whispers it, a mantra barely audible beneath her breath, as two traders crash together beside her. Their wares scatter across the frozen street—a cascade of metal trinkets, ration packs, and desperation. A flailing arm slices into her periphery. She ducks left, quick, sharp, instinct taking over where thought can't follow. Years of survival sharpened into reflex. Her world narrows to a tunnel—just the path ahead. Just escape.

Out.

She needs out.

The mouth of an alley yawns before her like salvation. Ceige slips into its shadows and presses herself against the icy wall, the rough brick biting through her jacket. Her breath comes in clouds, ragged and sharp, each exhale stolen by the frigid air. The darkness folds around her like a shroud—comforting for a heartbeat, then suffocating.

She doesn't linger.

Voices hum in her memory—low and warning, every word etched with urgency. The intel. Eira's experiments. The disappearances no one reports to police but everyone fears. Ceige feels them now as something visceral—a knot twisting deep inside her gut that tightens with every revelation.

Ceige understands why someone put a hit on her, and why, by accepting, she is now a marked woman.

"Focus." Her voice cuts through her own thoughts like a blade snapping against stone. She shakes her head, once, hard enough to sting.

No time for ghosts now. She's a hired killer, not a snoopy old lady holding a pity party.

Ceige pushes off the wall and starts moving again, boots crunching over snow packed down like brittle glass beneath her weight. The cold hits deeper with every breath she draws—the kind that works its way under your skin and stays there. Overhead, Cryosium looms: skeletal towers clawing at the starless sky like frozen ribs sheltering nothing but rot.

She weaves through the labyrinth of streets, narrow corridors twisting in on themselves like some cruel joke meant to trap souls too stubborn or stupid to leave this city behind. The ice-slick alleys feel endless—turn after turn until they blur into one indistinguishable maze of frost and shadow.

Footfalls echo.

Noise fades.

Steps slow.

Then she sees it.

Her safe house waits where it always does—a nondescript door shoved between two crumbling husks of buildings leaning on each other like exhausted drunks in their final moments of strength. Ceige pauses at the threshold, glancing back over her shoulder. The alley is empty.

Still hunted.

Ceige reaches into her pocket.

The key is gone.

Ceige's fingers scrabble through the pocket of her jacket. Then the other. Then her pants. Nothing. Just ammunition, a folded blade, a gun—worthless.

She yanks off the jacket, throws it to the floor. Shakes it hard, like trying to rattle loose its secrets. Hidden seams surrender knives and coins with metallic clinks, but not what she needs. Not the key.

Her breath comes shallow now, panic clawing its way up her throat. She drops to her knees, tearing through the gear she'd dumped in a corner after the escape—magazines, a shredded strap, a bent comm link—but no sign of that tiny sliver of metal and that carries her safety.

Her mind spirals back through the night—the enforcers, the Judex, boots pounding behind her, shots flying over her. Back further. She can still feel the hard weight of the key in her pocket, just before—

Ceige slams a fist against the wall, curses spilling from her lips like broken glass. There is only one answer: she'd lost it during the tryst.

Which means she'd lost it in *there*.

The thought hits her like cold steel slicing across bare skin. All those locks she'd bypassed, all those guards she'd slipped past like a shadow...

Her own safe house—too safe. Meant to be unbreakable, even with her X-9. xxx

The ghosts murmur warnings—they always do—but tonight she doesn't care what they think or what they want from her anymore because peace died long ago out there in Cryosium's icy veins alongside countless nameless others whose only crime was daring to live beneath its weight.

Tonight isn't about peace anyway.

It's about money.

She gathers what little she has without hesitation, then steps back into Cryosium's night embrace where shadows wait like old friends eager for secrets best left buried deep beneath ice too thick for sun or warmth or mercy ever to touch again.

It is time to return to Eiskorp, grab the flash drive she saw, and drive a stake through the heart of the monster.

Chapter 4

2:07 a.m.

"All according to plan," Ceige says.

Duck and roll.

Ceige moves through Eiskorp's halls, silent as smoke. Shadows cling to her boots, the corridors breathing with the soft hum of unseen machinery. Her heart pounds—steady, relentless—a metronome counting down the seconds.

The flash drive is waiting for her.

Proof.

It'll expose everything: Eira's secret experiments, her underground playground of human splicing and augmentation, lives torn apart for progress wrapped in profit. The thought should steady Ceige, but her fingers drift to the empty pocket where her key should be.

Gone.

Just like it was hours ago. That slip of metal has haunted her since she noticed its absence. Somewhere inside these walls, it waits to betray her—her safe house compromised if it falls into the wrong hands. If someone finds it... if they trace it back to her...

Focus.

She forces herself forward, slipping around a corner. Her pulse quickens—not fear, no, something else entirely. The hunt sharpens her senses; adrenaline thrums in her veins like music. Overhead, a red light blinks—a taunt stitched into steel and glass.

The camera watches.

Ceige's hand moves without hesitation, pulling the NeuroPick X-9 from its sheath at her hip. The tool gleams in her gloved hand—compact, elegant, deadly. It hums under her fingers like a living thing begging to be unleashed.

"Time to play," she whispers.

Her fingers flit across its controls, punching in a swift sequence that feels almost instinctive. The camera falters—one blink of its red eye before it dies entirely. The shadows deepen around her as the hall returns to silence.

She doesn't stop moving—even for a moment. Steps retraced with precision bring her closer to where she first saw it: an office door on the left, right where the administrative section begins to curve inward like some great beast's ribcage. This part of Eiskorp has shifted since then—small changes only employees would notice—but Ceige's map remains etched in her mind like stone.

The flash drive is there.

Or it had better be.

But something catches the light—a glint beneath a desk just paces away from her objective. Metallic and sharp-edged against the dim glow of emergency lighting.

Her breath catches.

The key lies half-hidden under a tangle of wires and dust—a small but vital thing misplaced yet waiting for discovery. Relief surges through her chest like cold water poured over flames, but she doesn't let it slow her down or weaken her focus.

She retrieves it swiftly—silent as ever—and slides it back into its rightful place: safety restored, sanctuary waiting for when this is over.

Then forward again.

The drive is close now—her real target: compact justice made from ones and zeros. Eira's death warrant sits in that office sitting at someone's carelessly ignored machine—so close she can feel its presence pulling at every step she takes toward finishing this mission once and for all.

Innocuous.

Average.

There.

Stuck in some desktop computer like it contains nothing more than last month's office supply list.

This is how empires fall, Ceige thinks—their secrets turned against them by their own hubris.

She reaches for the drive when—

BAM.

The door explodes inward with sudden violence—a crash of steel on plaster that reverberates through the room like gunfire. Glass rattles in their frames; papers scatter into flightless chaos across every surface like panicked doves caught mid-rest.

Adrenaline slams into Ceige's bloodstream like a shot of electricity. She quickly pockets the drive.

"Nice of you to drop in!"

Sloane's voice slices through the chaos—sharp-edged and laced with mockery as sweet as poison sugar. Her wild curls bounce with each swaggering step into the room; eyes glittering bright with danger and mischief collide with Ceige's own for one charged moment before anything else can fall apart further into madness.

"This is my kill. Get out of my way."

The lie tastes bitter on Ceige's tongue.

Two wolves, same den. Circling. Neither willing to bare their throat.

"Not happening," Sloane snaps, and then they lunge.

The collision isn't human—it's primal. A savage dance, years of training coiled in every strike, every dodge. Ceige moves first—a sidestep, fluid—and Sloane's already there, quick as a whip crack. Their hands meet in a clash of bone and muscle, the sterile hum of the office swallowed by the sound of impact. Glass crunches beneath their boots as they circle, the battlefield born from fluorescent sterility.

"Guess we're doing it the hard way," Ceige snarls, breath sharp-edged and jagged.

"Always love hurting you." Sloane's grin flashes like a blade—wicked, hungry—but her eyes betray her. There's something there. Something raw. A need to bury the past with each strike.

And Ceige? She feels the flash drive in her pocket like it's welded to her skin—so light it could dissolve into nothingness, but carrying the weight of everything she can't afford to lose.

Sloane emerges from shadow like a predator—fluid grace carved from endless reps on countless mats. A slow prowl into the dim half-light where emergency fluorescents sputter out their last gasps. Their eyes meet across the wreckage of an office left behind by people who don't matter anymore: desks turned barricades; chairs smashed to ruin.

"You know I want that," Sloane says softly—but her voice cuts like steel wire.

"And you know I can't trust you."

Ceige shifts her stance—weight low, steady—mapping angles, calculating outcomes even as her heart thunders against her ribs.

They explode into motion.

Sloane's fist carves through air and skims Ceige's jaw; Ceige ducks low and drives up with an uppercut that finds only empty space because Sloane moves like smoke—impossible to pin down for long enough to hurt her. Every motion feels rehearsed but unpredictable—all their strategies honed together now turned against one another.

A high kick whistles past Ceige's ear; she spins with it, snatching up a desk lamp mid-motion and swinging without thought but with perfect precision. The lamp explodes against drywall as Sloane weaves aside and closes the distance faster than Ceige can counter.

And then they clash again—sharp elbows, driving knees—a brutal brawl pulled tight around them like a noose. Close quarters means raw violence: no time to think, just react before pain or worse can find its way inside your defenses.

Blood stings hot as it drips from a gash above Ceige's brow; her arms burn from blocking Sloane's relentless blows—each one ringing down like crashing steel girders—but she doesn't fold because she *can't.* Cold conviction drives her forward where skill alone might fail.

They break apart.

Breaths too loud in the silence between strikes.

The emergency lights flicker overhead, throwing twisted shadows onto shattered tiles—a warped reflection of two bodies circling each other like orbiting moons about to collide again. The light hits Sloane's face: controlled breathing masking something deeper—a tremor in her stance Ceige catches because she knows *everything.* An old knee injury flaring up under pressure.

"Remember Budapest?" Sloane asks suddenly—the words just loud enough to reach across the space between them.

It hits harder than any punch could've managed.

Ceige doesn't answer—not with words—but something inside twists sharp enough to bleed anyway. Budapest presses its ghostly weight against her ribs while the floor tilts beneath old promises broken too many times over.

She uses it instead—the ache—and launches herself forward with a ferocity born from necessity more than anger now. The combination spills out automatically—a pattern memorized alongside Sloane's heartbeat back when trust wasn't just another weapon you learned how to wield or defend against.

But at the last second?

She changes it.

Her elbow arcs not toward where *Sloane expects*—the throat—but veers upward into temple instead: sharp bone meeting soft skin with sickening finality that reverberates through both bodies simultaneously.

Sloane staggers.

A flicker of surprise—there, then gone.

She's fast. Faster than most. But not fast enough.

Ceige doesn't hesitate. Her knee drives upward, forcing Sloane to block low. The feint works, and Ceige's elbow comes down hard, cracking solidly against the base of Sloane's skull.

"Why are you here?" Ceige snarls, closing the distance, her fist slamming into Sloane's ribs with a force that reverberates up her arm.

Sloane reels but answers with a kick—a vicious, precise strike that sends Ceige sprawling. "To settle a score," she spits, breathless but steady. "And maybe pull you into the abyss with me."

Ceige smirks, wiping blood from her lip with the back of her hand. "Like hell." The words are sharp, cutting through the tension like a blade. But beneath them—thrumming just beneath her skin—is a shiver she can't quite shake. Adrenaline. Their connection—a thread tangled with violence and something far more dangerous.

"Not exactly fair odds," Sloane taunts, circling now—a predator closing in on its prey. She moves like smoke, fluid and shifting.

"Fair doesn't exist," Ceige says, her voice low and steady as she mirrors Sloane's movements. Muscles coiled tight. Focus narrowing to a single point.

Then it happens.

A click.

Both stop moving.

Heads snap up as one.

Something shifts—a mechanism awakened—a trap sprung from the darkness.

The alarm screams to life—a jagged wail ripping through their frozen moment. Red light floods the room, drowning them in its harsh glow as steel shutters groan to life, grinding downward like a slow executioner's blade.

"Shit!" Sloane barks, bravado cracking under the weight of panic; it cuts across her face like lightning through storm clouds.

"Together?" Ceige asks quietly—too quiet for the chaos around them—her eyes fixed on Sloane's wild green gaze. Gauging. Weighing.

Sloane hesitates; her lips curl into something between a sneer and surrender. "Fine," she growls through gritted teeth, venom lacing every syllable. "But this isn't over."

"Deal," Ceige says curtly. No space for pride now—only survival. "Move."

They don't look at each other again; there isn't time.

The room becomes motion—blurring lines of shadow and flame-hued light as they carve through the space.

The dynamic shifts—the dance changes steps—and for an instant... they move as one.

No words pass between them now—only instinct and necessity binding them in fleeting unity amid the storm's roar.

"Keep up!" Sloane snaps over her shoulder—her voice cutting through the chaos like breaking glass—but there's an edge there that wasn't before: adrenaline laced with laughter, reckless and raw.

Ceige feels herself smile despite everything—the curve of her lips alien in this moment built from fire and fracture—but warmth touches her briefly nonetheless before vanishing again into cold resolve. Sloane has memorized the layout.

The building groans—a wounded beast threatening collapse—and they run together through twisting hallways bathed in blood-red light; shadows chase their heels as doors slam behind them with finality.

Through Eira's labyrinth they go—silent ghosts leaving no trace but whispers clinging stubbornly to walls trembling beneath impending ruin.

The frost-laced windows catch moonlight slicing sharp through glass fractures; it dances on broken floors below where secrets once rested safe until now—until them.

Their steps falter for only moments at a time before finding rhythm again: predators forced into uneasy alliance by something greater than themselves yet smaller somehow than the weight pressing down around them both.

The footsteps pound.

Relentless. Ominous.

They're coming, Ceige knows. And they won't be friendly.

The corridor hums with their approach—a pulsing rhythm of pursuit, inescapable as a predator's heartbeat. She feels their presence closing in, the air thick with inevitability.

They've danced to this tempo before, her and Sloane. A desperate duet, each step choreographed by necessity and survival.

"Now!" Ceige hisses, the word cutting through the stale air like a blade. They break into a sprint. Boots hammering against dead steel, each impact throwing up echoes that ricochet like war cries through the hollow passages.

The map. The doors. The exits.

Her mind claws at the details, dragging them from memory's recesses and pinning them in place with brutal clarity. They don't have time for mistakes.

"Follow my lead," she says, adrenaline surging like molten iron through her veins. She spots it—a hatch ahead, recessed into the wall like a secret passage waiting to be claimed. It's an old maintenance shaft, unused for years. Rust clings to its edges like scabs on a wound. It could lead anywhere—down into hell or up to salvation.

But it's all they've got.

"Hope you know where that goes!" Sloane calls behind her, her voice breathless but sharp-edged with that maddening self-assurance of her. She smirks—always smirking—even now, when death snaps at their heels like a feral dog.

For just an instant—just one—Ceige feels the warmth of it bleed past her defenses. That infuriating grin, reckless and unshakable, cuts through the icy knot coiled in her chest.

"Trust me," she bites out, not breaking stride as she slams into the hatch. The metal groans in protest as she wrenches it open, muscle and fury forcing compliance where finesse would fail.

The void yawns beneath them—black and unmeasured. No choice now.

They leap.

The darkness devours them whole, pulling them down into its cold embrace. The world narrows to the rattle of their breaths and the screech of boots against rungs as they descend into uncertainty's open mouth.

In this plunge—this shared chaos—they find something that wasn't there before. An unspoken bond forged in fear and desperation, tempered by survival's cruel fire. For just a moment—a fleeting heartbeat—it shields them from Eira's empire and the frostbite cruelty waiting outside these walls.

The ladder ends abruptly at another grate above them; Ceige doesn't hesitate as she pushes it free and pulls herself through with practiced efficiency.

Her feet hit steel again—a narrow passageway lit by weak, flickering strips of light that sputter like dying candles overhead.

"Left." She spits the word without hesitation as they reach an intersection, instincts slicing through options with surgical precision. She veers left; Sloane follows close on her heels without question or pause—the trust between them sharp-edged and unspoken.

Shadows coil around them like smoke, thrown wild across the walls by the failing fluorescents above. The space feels tight here—air compressed between metal plates that seem ready to collapse inward at any moment.

"Remind me again why we're not just burning this place to ash?" Sloane growls between gasps of breath; even now her voice carries a spark of humor beneath its serrated edge.

Ceige doesn't look back. "Because we only kill targets," she fires over her shoulder—each word clipped and cold as Cryosium's winter wind outside these walls. "Not every goddamn person on payroll."

It's not anger—it's focus carved down to its purest point—but it cuts just the same. Sloane doesn't reply; she doesn't need to. There's understanding in her silence—a grim acknowledgment of lines neither will cross... until they have to.

A disabled camera hangs slack on its mount as they pass—a dead eye watching nothing now—and Ceige feels the weight lift slightly from her shoulders. One less thing between them and freedom.

"Almost there," she mutters under her breath—not to Sloane but to herself—as if saying it aloud will make it true.

Her mind vaults ahead of her body now: calculating turns, memorizing distances, picturing escape routes where none exist yet but must soon be carved out by force or luck or both.

The corridor stretches ahead—the sterile metal swallowing sound except for their footfalls and ragged breathing—and somewhere beyond that final turn lies the bite of Cryosium's winter wind: merciless but honest compared to what waits behind them here inside these walls.

"Almost there," Ceige whispers, the words barely more than frost on her breath. Her mind pushes forward, racing to reach the exit before they do. Outside, Cryosium's winter waits. A predator crouched in the dark, its jaws of ice and wind eager to close around them. Behind her, the metal corridors stretch cold and sterile, the buzz of alarms fading under layers of iron and distance.

"Your 'almost' feels like a bad joke," Sloane says, a ragged laugh slipping through her panting breath. There's a glint in her voice—wild and electric, defiance sparking like flint against steel. Ceige hears it and feels it too, a pull deep in her chest. Fear tangled with something sharp and unspoken.

"Keep moving," Ceige snaps. She rounds the corner, muscles screaming for relief she refuses to give. The emergency exit looms ahead like a promise wrapped in fluorescent glare.

"After you, fearless leader," Sloane smirks, mischief dancing in the lines of her face even now.

"Shut up." But Ceige can't help herself; the corner of her mouth curves upward despite the pounding in her chest. She slams into the door shoulder first—it bursts open—and winter swallows them whole.

The wind doesn't just hit; it tears them asunder. Bitter and biting, slicing through layers of fabric to find skin. Snow swirls around their feet like restless ghosts, shrouding the path forward in shifting white.

"You've got such a goddamn mouth," Sloane mutters, voice half-swallowed by the wind. Her breath rises in curling plumes as she speaks—smoke dissipating into nothingness. But she doesn't stop scanning the street, eyes darting to shadows that stretch too long under dim streetlights.

"Move." Ceige doesn't wait for a response. One step into the snow leads to another—boots crunching against ice with a weight that feels heavier than it should. Soon to be covered by snow. The city yawns open before them—a sprawling labyrinth of dark streets and deeper secrets. The kind of place where survival is an unspoken prayer and every corner hides something waiting to pounce.

"Which way?" Sloane asks now. No teasing this time—just sharp edges and focus cutting through her voice like razors through silk.

"East." Ceige doesn't hesitate. "Hit the alley, keep low, head for the docks." Her mind maps it out as she speaks—lines drawn through frozen terrain like fault lines waiting to crack. Memories rear their heads—brief flashes from old missions gone wrong—but she forces them back down into silence.

Sloane nods once, quick and clipped. "Got it."

Their pace syncs without thought or question—as if they've done this a thousand times before or maybe not even once but it doesn't matter now because survival has no learning curve. Breath mingles between them in clouds that dissipate too quickly, leaving only frost and urgency behind.

They disappear into the night together—a pair of shadows moving fast through a city built on frostbitten silence and jagged edges. Every step forward cuts against Ceige like glass but stitches something else together: two borrowed lives caught in desperation's grasp, bound tighter by adrenaline than anything else could manage.

For now—just for now—they run as one.

"Don't slow me down."

Ceige's voice is a blade, cutting through the frost-laden air. Razor-sharp, steady. Unwavering. It doesn't betray the flicker inside her chest—the spark she doesn't dare name.

This alliance is nothing but a mirage, fragile and fleeting. But for now, survival binds them. Ghosts tethered to ghosts, slipping through Cryosium's icy veins with no room for sentiment.

At the end of the alley, Ceige pivots. The wind claws at her exposed skin, sharp as knives. She glances back—just a flash—but Sloane is there. Steady. Like a dog.

Snow falls thick now, swallowing everything it touches, burying their tracks in little white graves. Clean slate. Just how Ceige likes it. No footprints. No ties.

Her boots crunch against frozen ground as she sprints through a winding corridor of crumbled concrete and frost-coated steel. The city hums around her—a distant echo of sirens, whispers folded into the night, footsteps skimming across ice-slick pavement. Ceige keeps her head low, breath fogging in silver clouds that sting with every exhale.

Her legs carry her faster than her mind can keep up—or maybe it's her mind racing ahead now, caught on the weight in her pocket. The flash drive presses against her side like an iron brand growing heavier by the second. Eira won't forgive this betrayal, Ceige knows that much for certain—but somehow the thought unfurls a smirk across her lips.

The narrow path narrows further before yawning open into another passageway streaked with pale light dripping from a flickering streetlamp overhead. The pavement glimmers beneath it like black glass while shadows coil and slither in some grotesque dance beneath its eerie glow.

Phantoms twisting.

Breathing.

She pauses there—just for a moment—and lets adrenaline seep into her bones like poison and fire mingled in equal measure. The thrill tastes electric in the back of her throat: danger humming louder than heartbeats or sirens or snow-soft silence around her.

This is what she lives for.

But tonight, something else gnaws at the edge of that sensation—a whisper that doesn't belong to this moment but bleeds into it anyway: fierce eyes burning against hers; Sloane's voice coiling tight enough to suffocate—words laced with venomous promises.

She bursts forward.

Cold wind slashes at her face, bites at her skin. Her heart hammers, each beat a drum of defiance, urging her on. Survival. Freedom. Maybe—just maybe—an end to the solitude that clings to her like frost on stone.

The alleys twist and coil around her, the city a frozen labyrinth. Ceige spares a quick glance upward. Cryosium looms above, its spires slicing into the clouds like daggers of ice. Majestic, yes—but crushing. The weight of it bears down, heavy as the corruption that bleeds through its streets. Yet here, in the shadows, she breathes easier. Here, in the cracks and filth, she is untouchable.

She skids to a halt at the doorway—familiar, safe. Sloane lags behind, her shadow flickering into view just seconds too late. Fingers scrape metal. Key—her key—old fashioned and unhackable—slides into the lock; a twist and a click shatter the silence. The door yawns open, swallowing them whole.

Chapter 5

The air leaves bite marks.

Cold and sharp, it cuts into Ceige's lungs as she steps through the threshold. The safehouse greets her like a fist to the face—stale, metallic, reeking of rust and rot. Frost claws at the walls, jagged veins snaking over surfaces like the city's frozen arteries. The floor is cracked, fractured like old bones left too long in the cold. Scattered across the tables are remnants of failed ambitions—obsolete tech, wires coiled like dead snakes, dust-buried consoles blinking weakly in final surrender.

A graveyard of lost plans.

"Cozy," Sloane murmurs from behind her. Her voice is warm, almost teasing, but too close. Always too close. The heat radiating from her body—alive and pulsing—is an intrusion Ceige doesn't want. Not here. Not now.

Ceige doesn't answer. She pulls the flash drive from her pocket instead—a small, unassuming thing that feels heavier than it should. Secrets have weight. She knows this better than most. Sliding it into the holoscreen's port, she watches as blue light spills out, harsh against the dimness. It stretches and climbs up the frost-covered walls, casting shadows that jitter and shift like trapped phantoms.

"What's on it?" Sloane asks, stepping nearer still, her breath brushing Ceige's neck with unwanted warmth. It sends a ripple through her nerves—small but sharp—and she fights the instinct to recoil.

"Answers," Ceige says flatly, her eyes locked on the screen as the decryption software begins its work. Strings of code flood the display in chaotic streams. "Something Eiskorp doesn't want anyone to see."

Sloane laughs softly—low and reckless—like she has all the time in the world to waste. "If we even live long enough to care."

"Shut up and focus," Ceige snaps without turning. But her own focus is slipping; she can feel it fray under Sloane's proximity and the suffocating tension building in the room.

The decryption stops.

Her pulse jerks in response—a drumbeat trapped inside her ribs—and for a moment, the air around them thickens into something alive, something pressing down on them both.

"Don't keep me waiting," Sloane whispers, leaning close enough for their shoulders to touch now. A small spark ignites where they meet: heat against cold; chaos against restraint.

"Patience," Ceige grits out through clenched teeth.

The screen flickers again.

And it picks up—slow at first, then faster—as fragments of data emerge from darkness into electric blue clarity. Lines of text spill onto the holoscreen like jagged confessions ripped from a guilty throat: rows of clinical documentation cataloging human experiments conducted on LaFayette Street residents.

Ceige squints at the words swimming before her eyes while frost seems to thicken around them—the room colder now somehow despite Sloane's heat beside her.

The world narrows.

Everything outside this room dissolves into nothingness as Ceige stares at what they've uncovered: horrors carved into sterile reports.

"Are we seeing this?" Sloane's voice, brittle. A whisper that shatters against the dark. Shadows crawl. Deepen. The corners of the room disappear, devoured whole. Ceige feels Sloane's gaze. A brand. Burning her skin.

"Shhh." Sharper than a blade. Ceige can't afford to falter. Not now, not ever. The screen flickers, alive with horrors that gnaw at the edges of her mind, threatening to tear it apart. Neural enhancements. Muscle density experiments. "Terminations." Neat little word for what they do—lives reduced to numbers on a ledger, disposable as spoiled rations.

Her voice hardens, steeling against the bile rising in her throat as she reads: "'Project Ascension converts society's 'undesirables' into enhanced military assets through neural rewiring and genetic modification. Success rate: 27%. Benefits include tripled strength and accelerated healing. Current challenges: high mortality rate and post-conversion lifespan of .7 years.'" Each word like acid on her tongue. "'Subjects sourced primarily from rehabilitation centers and homeless shelters.'"

"Goddamn." Sloane leans closer, breath brushing against Ceige's shoulder, warm against the cold that seeps into the bones of the safehouse. "They're turning people into weapons"

Weapons. For a war no one wins. Ceige doesn't look at her, doesn't blink, doesn't let herself feel anything but anger.

"That's the military-industrial complex," she mutters past the knot in her throat. Her fingers tighten on the edge of the desk. This is what they're fighting—a machine that grinds people down to pulp and molds what's left into monsters. But she won't break now.

The documents unfurl before her, line after line of rot and ruin spilling out, every click another betrayal she forces herself to commit. Military contracts flash like gunfire across the screen—cold promises scrawled out in ink and blood: enhanced "urban pacification units," memory suppression protocols. Soldiers stripped of souls, obedient puppets on strings.

"Ceige…" Sloane's voice quivers, thick with something raw and jagged, words breaking apart in the frozen air between them.

"Keep it together." Ceige forces her voice steady even as she feels cracks spidering through old walls inside herself, threatening collapse. She glances at Sloane—eyes burning with fire and brimming with sorrow—and wonders if this is where it all falls apart for them too.

"We need a way to stop it," she says, holding tight to resolve stretched thin enough to snap at any second. "Evidence? Maybe…"

"Video evidence? Of… this?" Sloane nods toward the screen but keeps her distance from it—as if proximity might burn her alive too—or worse, pull her in completely. She laughs then, hollow as an empty graveyard wind: "Yeah, I'm sure that'll hold up great in court."

"Exactly." Ceige spits out a grin that isn't really a grin at all; a mask stretched taut over something crumbling inside her chest. "You think they give a damn about legality?"

The room answers for Sloane.

Footage rolls. Grainy video feeds claw their way onto the screen like ghosts from some forgotten hellscape—figures twisted beyond recognition move with impossible speed and strength before collapsing like broken toys tossed aside by cruel hands.

Ceige stares.

Her stomach churns as images drill themselves into her memory: veins glowing under pale skin slick with sweat; bodies convulsing until there's nothing left but silence; faces empty as death claims them one by one.

She closes her eyes—not to look away but to let it sink in.

"Here," Sloane murmurs.

Soft. Broken. A voice splintered by disbelief.

The screen shifts, its glow cutting through the cold darkness of the safehouse. Documents flash into view, stamped with Eiskorp's insignia—a logo sharp as a blade, glinting with malice.

"New Hope Recovery Center." Sloane's voice falters, the words heavy on her tongue. "They're using these people—"

"—like tools," Ceige finishes. The words scrape her throat, jagged and bitter. She feels it crack, that armor she wears so carefully, fractures spreading beneath the surface like ice under pressure. This isn't just another mission. This is devastation disguised as progress. A betrayal that feeds on despair.

"Look at this." Sloane's finger trembles over a chart. "Breaking them down, piece by piece." Her voice rises, trembling with fury barely restrained. "Like they're nothing."

Her fist clenches—the tension coiling tight—a spring primed to snap.

"This is sick. 'Subject unwilling.' 'Subject resistant.'"

"Welcome to Eiskorp," Ceige says flatly, but the words are hollow, collapsing in her mouth like ash. She turns away, lets the shadows wrap themselves around her like armor. Hiding what shouldn't show.

The screen flickers again, spilling more files like spilled blood across the room.

Ceige scans quickly, her eyes darting over data points and charts until one stops her cold: a name buried under layers of sterile jargon.

Ginger Vale.

Sloane's sister.

A "resistant" participant.

The word lands like shrapnel.

"Fuck." The curse falls out of Sloane's mouth—raw and jagged, carved out of rage and grief.

Ceige doesn't need to look to know Sloane's hands are fists now, knuckles pale as bone. Doesn't need to look to feel the realization crashing over her like ice water poured from a great height.

"No..." A whisper. A wound laid bare.

"Stay calm," Ceige says instinctively as she reaches for her partner—but Sloane already spins toward the screen, tears slipping free in defiance of strength worn too long in place of armor.

"She didn't want this!" Each word breaks smaller than the last—splinters flying apart as she speaks them out loud to no one but herself. "They used her!" Her breath hitches—anger turning brittle under the weight of grief brought back into sharp focus like daggers watching from shadows lingering too close now closer still...

"God...they took everything! From me! From *her!*"

Ceige's heart pounds.

Not just fear. Not just dread. Something sharper.

Across the room, Sloane unravels. A storm, torn apart by its own winds—fury and grief colliding into something raw and jagged. Ceige hadn't thought it possible. To see her like this. The woman who never flinched, trembling under the weight of whatever hell she'd just dredged up.

The holoscreen flickers in front of her, lines of code crawling to their end. One last file decrypting—one final wound ready to split open. Ceige's fingers hover above the controls, cold sweat creeping down her back as the frostbitten air presses in on her chest. She watches the glyphs bleed across the screen until they stop. Complete. The truth staring back at them like a loaded gun.

She swipes her hand through the projection. The light dies immediately, plunging them into darkness.

She understood now, how she had been set up to take the job. Whoever bought her skills, bought her ethics. Morality. Consciousness.

They knew.

Part of the plan.

"Go home," she says—low, cutting. Her voice carves through the silence like a blade through ice. She doesn't look at Sloane anymore; can't bring herself to face the heat radiating off her frame—a furnace against the frozen void of this safehouse prison.

"Fuck that." Sloane steps forward, her shadow breaking against the faint glow clinging to the walls. Green eyes flash like distant lightning in a storm that refuses to quiet. "I'm not walking away from this."

"You're not thinking straight," Ceige says. Her jaw locks tight as she shifts her stance, trying to anchor herself before everything collapses around them both.

"Maybe I don't want to think straight." Sloane shoves her hands deep into her pockets, pacing now, caught somewhere between smoldering and erupting. "You think you can order me around? Like this isn't personal?"

"It's *too* personal," Ceige snaps back, sharp and brittle as cracking glass. "It clouds your judgment. Stop before..."

Sloane stops mid-step, glaring at her through the dim haze of shadowed light. "Before what?" she spits out, each word dripping with venom, with pain barely contained beneath it all. "Before I get myself killed? Is that what you're so worried about? Newsflash—I'd rather die doing something than run away like a coward." Her voice breaks—not weak but fierce, edged with something so raw it cuts deeper than any blade could.

Silence clings between them now, thick as smoke choking out air in a sealed room.

Ceige feels it—the truth she doesn't want to admit lodged like shrapnel in her chest. She can't argue with Sloane because she knows it too well; surrender might be their only fight left.

"Fine." The word slips from her lips before she can stop herself—an uneasy truce formed from desperation more than agreement.

"You want in?" Her tone hardens again as resolve roots itself where doubt had crept moments before. "Then we do this my way."

Sloane tilts her head slightly—half defiant smirk curving along lips that refuse anything resembling surrender or submission.

"Whatever you say," she quips back with fire barely restrained beneath mockery. "But I'm not backing down."

"Good." Ceige's face cracks—just a smirk, sharp and quick as a razor blade. "Don't forget who's in charge."

"Never." Sloane steps closer, the safehouse air folding between them. A challenge, quiet but loud enough to cut. The space is tense, electric, packed with something unsaid.

Ceige exhales, her breath floating pale and thin in the freezing air before vanishing into the shadows. Shadows that jitter across peeling walls crusted in frost. The cold seeps into her bones, but the real chill is inside her—a barricade she spent years building, brick by stubborn brick. Now it starts to crack.

"I…" Sloane's voice snaps through the room like a whip, yanking Ceige out of her thoughts. There are tears in Sloane's eyes—they catch the faint light and cut deeper than they should. They slice right through what Ceige keeps locked up inside.

"Come here," Ceige says. It's not a plea—it's an order. The words taste strange in her mouth, foreign and unwelcome. They feel like stepping into a void so dark it might swallow her whole.

For a second, Sloane hesitates. Just a second too long. It makes something twist hard and sharp in Ceige's chest, but then Sloane moves. She crosses the distance with all the weight of inevitability and crashes into Ceige like a wave hitting rock. Tactical gear rustles against fabric; warmth replaces frost.

Sloane shakes against Ceige's shoulder—her voice muffled but clear enough to reach where it hurts most: "Don't tell me to leave again."

Ceige swallows down everything she wants to say and picks something else—something sharp-edged to keep them both standing. "You'll never get your revenge if you fall apart out there."

The words come steady, strong enough to hold up walls even as they crumble inside her, but they're wasted breath, both of them know it. Sloane isn't going anywhere.

"Fuck that." Sloane pulls back just enough for Ceige to see what burns behind tear-glistened lashes—the fire of someone who refuses to be snuffed out. "I'd rather die than let you go out there alone."

"Then die awake," Ceige fires back just as quickly—words like sparks striking steel—and regrets nothing when she sees how Sloane lights up at the challenge. That fire is real now, crackling between them: part hope, part dread.

"I—"

"Shut up," Ceige cuts her off before she can finish whatever reckless thing was about to fall from her lips. Without thinking—or maybe after thinking too much—she cups Sloane's face in one rough hand. Her thumb brushes away one tear as it trails down skin that feels almost too warm under her touch.

Sloane freezes for half a breath before whispering: "Ceige..."

It isn't much of a word—just a name caught between fear and something softer—but that doesn't stop Ceige from leaning in anyway. Their lips meet—not hard or fast or desperate—but soft and unsure, testing instead of taking.

It's nothing.

It's everything.

A moment suspended in frost and fire—a fragile truce carved out of chaos—with no promise it will hold longer than this breath between them.

"Jesus."

The word tumbles from Sloane's lips, soft, startled. She pulls back, her breath hitching, eyes wide as if caught in the glare of something too bright, too raw. Vulnerability etches itself across her face—a fragile crack in the armor she wears so well.

Ceige doesn't flinch. Doesn't move. Her voice stays low, steady as bedrock: "Don't overthink it."

She cups Sloane's face in her hands, their foreheads pressed together like a vow neither dares to speak aloud. The cold clings to them, seeps into the marrow of their bones like some parasitic thing—but here, between them, warmth flickers. Blooms. A fragile ember defying frost.

Sloane huffs a weak laugh. "Like you never do?" she teases, or tries to—but there's no real sharpness in it. Just a thin smile stretched over something softer—something that makes Ceige's chest tighten until it aches.

Ceige leans in again. This time slower. This time sure. Their lips meet and linger—hesitation unraveling into something deeper, something heavier. This isn't just a kiss; it's an unspoken confession—a laying bare of all the hurt and all the need and all the years they've spent choking on things left unsaid.

Each brush of their lips tastes of old scars and unforgotten horrors—their pasts heavy ghosts settling between them—but beneath it all is something sharper, hotter: the mission that looms ahead like a storm gathering on the horizon.

The room around them reeks of mildew and neglect—rotted wood and damp concrete—but they carve out a corner for themselves amidst the decay. A sanctuary made not from stone walls but from touches and breath shared in defiance of everything outside these crumbling walls. Time stretches thin like pulled thread; just for now, there is no Eiskorp. No chaos waiting beyond the door. No war shivering on their horizon.

Ceige's fingers tremble as they find the straps of Sloane's tactical vest—hard buckles slick with frost biting into her fingertips as she fumbles with them one by one. Each click echoes sharply against the cold silence of the room—a reminder that the outside world is still there, waiting to devour them whole.

"Get my shit off," Sloane murmurs, grinning through half-lidded eyes, her voice colored with playful mischief—but even now Ceige can see it: that flicker of fragility beneath her bravado like paper stretched too thin against flame.

"Yeah," Ceige manages, forcing a smirk she'd forgotten how to wear until now—a mask poorly fitted over old wounds still bleeding beneath it. She pulls at the vest until it slides free from Sloane's shoulders, their bodies brushing faintly—heat meeting cold where skin meets fabric meets air so frozen it bites like teeth.

Her hand falters—just briefly—as her eyes catch on a line jagged across Sloane's forearm: pale scar tissue jagging cruelly over darkened skin like lightning etched into earth after rainstorms gone violent.

"Nice scar," Ceige says, her voice low, a fingertip brushing the jagged line carved into Sloane's forearm. The touch lingers, a whisper against the skin, and something stirs in her chest—a shiver rippling down her spine. "Didn't notice it before. New?"

Sloane's lips twitch, just barely. "Not that new." Her voice is quiet, softer than she meant it to be. "The usual mess."

Her green eyes glint—mischief lighting their depths—but there's something else there too. A question. A dare. It cuts deep enough to make Ceige hesitate, her exterior slipping for just a moment, enough to let out a slow breath as her fingers work free the last strap.

"Yes," Sloane answers before Ceige can ask. Their eyes lock, and for an instant, the world falls away—the mission, the cold city clawing at the windows, the weight of everything waiting just outside these walls. None of it exists here. Just them. Just this fragile, flickering moment stripped bare of pretense.

"Your turn." Ceige's voice is steady, but the air between them vibrates like a wire stretched too thin. The tension hums, electric and sharp. Sloane doesn't hesitate—her hands move fast, peeling back layers with methodical precision until Ceige stands exposed beneath her gaze: pale skin crisscrossed with scars and bruises, each etching a survival.

Sloane's fingers pause just above one mark, then drift lower, tracing it—not gently but deliberately—as if mapping terrain she plans to commit to memory. The stories woven into Ceige's flesh draw her in deeper than she expected. Weapons lie forgotten on the floor beside them now; steel and polymer discarded in soft clinks like relics at an altar. Trust offered in silence.

"Looks like we've both lived through some shit," Sloane murmurs at last. No tease this time; no sharp-edged smile to follow it up. Instead, her words settle heavy between them, as if acknowledging what they've survived is somehow heavier than bearing it alone ever was.

Ceige doesn't reply—not with words—but the pounding in her chest betrays her thoughts well enough: that these scars mean something more than pain or loss or shame. They mean survival—and maybe something even harder to face: hope.

The closeness stretches out like thread between them—fragile but unbroken—until Ceige finally exhales and breaks it herself with a half-smile tugging at the corner of her mouth.

"Bed," she mutters under her breath, reaching out to guide Sloane toward the makeshift cot tucked in the corner of their shelter—its rough fabric waiting to scrape against skin still warm from unspoken confessions.

Sloane allows herself to be led as though every step holds its own gravity—slow movements pulling against unseen currents—and when they drop onto the bed together it creaks softly beneath their weight; the sound swallowed by wind howling just outside these fragile walls.

For now, there is only this: two bodies suspended between war stories and warmth while shadows stretch long across their sanctuary like ghosts refusing to let go.

"Not so bad, huh?" Sloane sinks onto the mattress. Her smile cuts through the shadows—a flash of light in the gloom. Laughter spills out, soft and fleeting, but Ceige can feel the weight creeping back, heavy as the frost on the windows. The reminder that this moment is stolen, and nothing stolen ever lasts.

"Wait until morning," Ceige murmurs, leaning in. Her breath brushes Sloane's, warm in the icy air. Close enough to share it. Close enough to steal it back. "We've still got a job to do."

Sloane's eyes catch hers, glinting with something that almost looks like mischief—almost. "Always the pragmatist," she says, but her voice falters at the edges.

Ceige reaches out. Her fingers move like whispers over Sloane's bare skin—a silent conversation neither of them dares to speak aloud. The world beyond these walls fades into something unreal, a distant hum swallowed by the quiet here. Just them. Just this. Their breaths entwine, heavy with everything unspoken.

"Goddamn." Sloane's voice cracks open—raw, aching. She tilts her head back, baring her throat like an offering or a challenge. A dare wrapped in silk skin and fragile trust. Ceige takes it. Her hands move, deliberate and slow; every touch sparks fire in the cold room, flames flickering where their skin meets.

"Who knew you had such soft hands?" Sloane almost laughs—it's there in her tone—but something deeper swallows it before it can form fully.

"Shut up," Ceige mutters, her words stumbling out unsteady—half plea, half command. "Just... shut up."

Sloane doesn't laugh this time. She nods instead, her grin slipping into something smaller. Something softer. Vulnerable edges peeking through before she leans forward and closes the space between them again with a kiss—gentle at first, a question hanging on trembling lips. Then firmer, an answer written in warmth and saltwater.

Ceige's resolve falters beneath it—the pull of Sloane's hands threading through her hair like anchors dragging her down into this fleeting moment where nothing else matters. Not the storm clawing at the roof above them. Not the mission waiting just beyond dawn's edge.

Just this.

Just Sloane.

The cold presses against their sanctuary like a predator circling prey, but here inside it doesn't reach them—not when heat blooms between their bodies where they touch and crash together.

"You're not freezing now," Sloane whispers against Ceige's lips. The words carry just enough playfulness to tug a laugh from somewhere deep in Ceige's throat—a low sound breaking through the quiet like shattering glass.

"No," Ceige admits softly as she shifts closer, hovering over Sloane now—like a shadow drawn to light too bright to resist. Her fingers move again along familiar terrain: tracing jawlines and collarbones as if etching each curve into memory one last time, carving permanence into something impermanent.

The lantern glows.

Soft light, soft shadows.

It casts their faces in gold and shadowplay, turning flickers into something too alive to be illusion. Their lips meet again, deeper now, hungrier. Sloane draws Ceige down onto the worn mattress, their bodies fitting together with an ease that feels stolen from a dream. Movements slow, deliberate. A quiet rebellion against time and fate—both pressing, both cruel.

Sloane's hand slides up Ceige's back and rests there, firm but trembling. Holding her in place as if she might dissolve into the smoke of a memory when morning comes. "Do you think," Sloane whispers between kisses, her breath catching as Ceige lets her lips wander down the curve of her neck, igniting ember trails on her skin, "that things will ever slow down for us? Just... long enough?"

Ceige stills. Lifts her head the barest fraction to meet Sloane's eyes. The rawness there—a fragile open wound—makes something inside Ceige twist and tighten. A vow she can't form into words rises in her throat instead. To protect this fragile moment. To protect Sloane.

"Maybe," she says at last, the word soft as smoke curling between them. Her hand moves, brushing a stray lock of hair back from Sloane's face like smoothing the wrinkles from an old photo. "But until they do... this? Right here? It's ours."

Sloane nods—slow, small—but it says everything before she tugs Ceige back down into another kiss. And this time it's surrender—no, salvation—as they drown together in the forgetting.

Ceige lets her lips trace along the edge of Sloane's jaw, slow as a river carving stone. Warm breath blooms against Sloane's skin as Ceige lingers just beneath her ear. A shiver ripples through Sloane—it takes root somewhere deep, growing outward in threads she can't untangle—and her fingers bury themselves in Ceige's hair. Dark rivers spilling over knuckles and through hands like liquid silk.

Their movements are steady but sure now—each touch purposeful, each stroke mapping out a territory they may never return to again but need to know by heart. The bed creaks beneath them—a faint protest—and anchors them to this small sliver of reality while the rest dissolves: danger waiting outside like wolves; jagged memories lurking just out of reach.

Ceige presses a knee against Sloane's thigh—not hard, just enough to beckon—and without hesitation Sloane shifts closer into that silent invitation. Her breath catches there, trapped on some invisible line between fear and want.

Ceige holds on.

Sloane falters, buckles under the weight pressing down—grief, fear, something heavier than either—but Ceige doesn't let her fall. Steadies her instead. Her hands move without pause—up shoulders, down arms—until fingers meet and twine with Sloane's. That connection hums louder than any kiss, speaks volumes in its quiet strength. Ceige squeezes, her grip firm but soft, grounding them both here in this fragile moment, as if the world beyond these walls has crumbled into silence.

The safehouse disappears. Peeling walls and splintered beams vanish beneath the heat that arcs between them.

Sloane exhales, a trembling breath against Ceige's cheek. She shifts closer, their legs tangling like ivy creeping through cracks in stone—slowly but inevitably. Ceige smiles into the next kiss, a faint curve of lips that Sloane feels more than sees. Their movements fall into rhythm, unhurried and sure, every touch deliberate yet edged with something teasing, as if time itself has stretched thin to give them this one brief eternity.

Sloane presses down at last. Yields to gravity. To instinct. Her weight sinking into Ceige's body with an inevitability that feels like surrender and salvation all at once. Her head dips low, lips grazing the sharp plane of Ceige's collarbone—a fleeting touch that sparks like static in dry air. Ceige arches beneath it, a gasp slipping free before she can rein it back, her fingers finding their way to the nape of Sloane's neck.

They move together—not hurried, not frantic—but seamless. As though they've danced this same dance a thousand times before yet still stumble across new steps with every shift of bare skin on bare skin. The tension doesn't snap all at once; it unwinds in waves. Slow, rolling currents that build and recede with every sigh caught between them, every press of fingertips on vulnerable flesh. Time bends around them; they don't rush it.

Outside, the city sinks deeper into nightfall. Distant neon glows faint and blue now where ochre had reigned before—slivered light filtering through cracks in boarded windows to paint cool shadows over their bodies locked in warmth. The contrast sharpens everything: Sloane's forehead resting against Ceige's shoulder in breathless quiet; Ceige's hand sweeping slow circles over Sloane's back when she shivers—not from cold but from something marrow-deep and undefinable.

The room grows colder; the air bites sharper through broken walls.

But here—where they lie entangled—it burns on.

The world is quiet now.

Their bodies still. Their pulses no longer hammering against the inside of their skin like trapped birds desperate to escape.

They lie tangled together, limbs an unsolved riddle that somehow makes perfect sense. Sloane's face presses into the curve of Ceige's neck, and when she hums, the sound vibrates low and soft, something too delicate to exist in a place like this. Ceige pulls the somewhat of a blanket higher with one hand, her other arm looping firm around Sloane's waist.

An anchor. A tether.

The weight of her holds Ceige here, keeps her from slipping away into whatever darkness waits beyond these walls.

Their breaths fill the small room in steady rhythm—soft exhales expanding into the silence left behind by words unsaid. Sloane's fingers trace over Ceige's skin, slow now, as sleep begins to claim her. The patterns she draws fade into stillness.

"Doesn't feel so bad, does it?" Sloane's voice is low, teasing, but there's something raw underneath it—a wonder she can't quite hide. Her green eyes catch what little light filters through the cracks in their shelter, glinting like shards of broken glass. She moves her hand across Ceige's arm again—light strokes over marks earned in blood and fire—as though each touch is a vow to remember all of it. To remember her.

Ceige keeps her gaze fixed on the ceiling, lets out a quiet snort that could almost pass for amusement. "Don't get used to it," she says. The words fall out sharp-edged but dull on impact. She threads her fingers through Sloane's wild curls instead, pauses when she feels their warmth against her hand.

It startles her sometimes—how close this feels to falling apart.

How close it feels to hope.

"We've got work to do."

Sloane exhales sharply through her nose—the beginning of a laugh that doesn't quite make it out intact. "Always all business with you, huh?" There's sarcasm on her tongue now, but it twists at the edges, softening too much for her usual bite to stay intact. "Can't you just sit still for once? Or do you have some world-class killing spree scheduled I wasn't informed about?"

"How about I breathe while you stop being a smartass?" Ceige counters without thinking. A smirk tugs at one corner of her mouth despite herself—it feels strange there, foreign—but Sloane catches it anyway. It makes her grin widen just a bit more than before.

For once—not forever but enough—the sharp things between them dissolve into echoes of laughter that split open something fragile in the air around them.

Sloane leans in close after that, their foreheads brushing together as she murmurs slow enough for Ceige to feel every word vibrate between them. "When this is over..." A pause hangs there like the edge of a blade waiting for its fall. "I'm taking you out for a drink." Something flickers in her eyes—something open and shattering all at once—and Ceige looks away before she can see too much of it.

"No Judex allowed," Sloane adds after a beat.

"Sounds like a plan," Ceige murmurs. Her voice is low, steady—a spark against the chill that clings to their skin like frost. The words linger in the air, brittle as ice, refusing to melt even in the fragile heat of their embrace. For now, they stay locked together, a tangled refuge built on desperation. And something else. Something softer.

Sloane shifts, her tone sharpening and softening all at once. "I'm not good at goodbyes."

"Then we won't say one," Ceige answers. The words feel heavier than they should, sinking too deep. Their bond is a thread stretched thin over chaos and ruin, but it holds.

For now. Maybe just for now. But Ceige grips it anyway, knowing it might break, knowing she'll hold on until it cuts her palm.

"Together then," Sloane says. Her voice is iron wrapped in fire, forged hard against the cold pressing in from outside. The city beyond them freezes and crumbles. The storm howls. But here—here in this fragile hollow—they burn, small but defiant, daring the dark to tear them apart.

Chapter 6

The cold daylight strikes.

A slap. Sharp, uninvited.

Ceige and Sloane step out of the sagging safe house, last night's stale heat clinging to them like a ghost they can't quite shake. Snow falls like ash from a funeral pyre, settling into cracks in the pavement's skin. They don't notice. Their eyes are too busy—sweeping, searching, reading the edges of shadows.

Sloane flicks her comm. The screen glows faintly, an ember in the gray: *"Alley north of Adamansky and Minner-amp. Eiskorp. I will talk."* No name. No signature. Doesn't need one. It's bait, and they're starved.

"An invitation," Ceige says, her voice low and flat, clipped like distant gunfire. Her hand brushes her gun, fingers tightening briefly on its grip—solid, certain, alive against her side. She glances up at Sloane. Something passes between them—quick, sharp-edged, impossible to pin down. Hunger? Fear? Maybe both.

"Let's not keep our friend waiting," Sloane murmurs, her lips twisting into that smirk—the one that dances the line between charm and ruin. It doesn't reach her eyes; those stay hard as cut glass. Together they move into the street, boots crunching over snow that clings to cracked asphalt like frostbitten veins.

The alley swallows them whole.

Walls streaked with grime rise on either side—narrow slabs of frostbitten concrete pressing in close as if trying to crowd them out or crush them flat. The wind slips through like a knife edge, a low whistle that carries the stink of rusted metal and burned-out dreams.

Ceige leans back against the frozen brick, her breath curling in pale plumes that dissolve too fast. Her gut twists—not fear exactly but something heavier and colder, weighing down every nerve. She watches Sloane move ahead, wild black curls bouncing as if mocking gravity itself. Defiant as ever. Reckless as always.

"Keep your head on," Ceige mutters under her breath—half warning, half prayer.

Sloane grins over her shoulder without slowing down, teeth flashing bright against the grime-stained gloom. "Me? Always sharp," she says lightly, then adds with a wink: "Just ask the corpses."

Her laugh cuts through the air—a bright shard of sound against all that oppressive silence—and Ceige almost smiles despite herself. Almost.

It's always this way when they hunt together—a sharp-edged rhythm neither can resist nor escape: chaos and precision colliding in perfect syncopation. Two jagged souls bound by violence and vengeance tighter than any chains.

But Sloane's recklessness—it gnaws at Ceige in ways she'll never admit aloud. Thrilling one moment; terrifying the next.

"All according to plan," Ceige snaps suddenly as they reach the edge of the alley where snow swirls like restless ghosts around their ankles. The humor evaporates from her tone as quickly as warmth vanishes into this biting air.

They pause at the threshold between shadowed alleyway and white-draped street beyond, peering out through veils of falling snow.

Waiting—for signs of movement. For whispers of betrayal.

For something worth killing before it kills them first.

The snow suffocates.

A white abyss, a frozen pall.

Cryosium doesn't kill with heat, Ceige thinks. It freezes you alive, steals your breath, buries you in its embrace.

Like Sloane.

She crouches by the jagged mouth of the alley, the cold gnawing through her layers. Around her, the city looms—a skeletal corpse draped in frost. The wind howls like a dying animal, and the snow swirls thick enough to choke. Somewhere in the haze, desperation stirs.

"Don't get all broody on me now," Sloane whispers, her voice a dry rasp against the storm. She elbows Ceige lightly, though her hand grips her weapon tight. "You'll scare him off before he even shows."

Ceige doesn't answer. Her blood beats slow but hot, every pulse sending fire through her veins. It's a trap or a turning point—nothing in between—but either way, it's here.

"There." Sloane nods toward the shifting shadows. A figure emerges—hunched and brittle against the wind's bite.

"Stay sharp," Ceige murmurs. She feels the familiar tension coil inside her like a predator before the pounce. The safety's already off; she doesn't remember flicking it.

Trust doesn't exist here. Not in Cryosium.

Everything is swallowed in white silence—the kind that strips sound away and leaves only dread behind. The snow flays at exposed skin, each flake sharp as glass. Ceige squints into it, searching for movement in the blur. Her breath clouds in front of her face, ghosting into nothingness.

"That's him," Sloane says from behind her, voice low but taut, cutting through the static air like wire snapping under strain.

Ceige nods once and steps forward—out of cover and into the open snowfield that masquerades as an alley. Her boots crunch against ice as she moves toward the figure emerging from the storm.

He stumbles closer—a man hollowed out by fear and frost. His shoulders sag beneath a ragged coat that flutters uselessly in Cryosium's merciless grip. His hands clutch a battered briefcase like it holds his soul or someone else's ransom. Each step looks heavier than the last—the weight of desperation dragging him down like an anchor through frozen seas.

"Keep watch," Ceige says over her shoulder without looking back at Sloane. The words are steel-edged, deliberate—the sound of control wrapped tight around chaos.

And then she calls out: "Friend!" Her voice cuts across the wind like a blade drawn clean from its sheath. Cold enough to carry weight but not yet enough to draw blood. Her weapon hangs loose at her side—calculated disarmament masking predatory intent.

The man freezes mid-step, head jerking up like prey caught in lamplight. His eyes dart wildly into shadows that aren't there but might as well be everywhere—for all he knows, this city breathes death from its cracks and corners.

"Yes," he stammers finally, his voice thin and trembling under Cryosium's icy press. Words spill fast, disjointed: "I—I have information... Eiskorp—they're—they can't know I'm here."

Behind Ceige comes Sloane's voice—laced with venom spun into silk: "You sure about this?" A question that isn't really a question at all—just a shard of mockery dressed as doubt.

Ceige glances back for only a moment—just long enough to catch Sloane's silhouette leaning against the wall like shadow melted into brickwork—and feels something warm flicker briefly beneath her ribs before it dissolves again into cold purpose.

Ahead of her, the whisteblower clutches his briefcase tighter and steps closer still... like a man holding onto hope while standing on thin ice above dark water.

The frost bites.

Sharp. Relentless.

It seeps into Ceige's bones as they wait, the cold air coiling around her like a snake. Sloane lingers behind her, a shadow etched into the darkness, her voice cutting through the silence like a razor.

"Are you sure you want to do this, friend?" The words drip with venomous humor, her tone an arrow aimed to wound. She doesn't move, doesn't need to. Chaos is Sloane's weapon, and she wields it with ease.

Ceige doesn't look back. Doesn't need to.

She knows Sloane is smiling.

Ahead of them, the man trembles. Fragile as glass, close to shattering. "M-my name is Niall," he stammers, his breath misting in the frigid air. "Niall O'Sullivan. Y-you don't understand."

The briefcase in his grip sways wildly, its weight threatening to pull him over. He takes a shaky step forward, knees buckling like a puppet on broken strings.

"They'll come for me if they find out I'm here!" His voice cracks. Panic leaks through every syllable.

"Who?" Ceige's voice lashes out, sharper than steel. She moves toward him, steps deliberate and measured. Her eyes rake over him, peeling back layers of skin and fear to find the truth buried beneath. "Who gave you her number?"

"Dark." He flinches at the name—not subtle enough to escape her notice. There's something ugly in his reaction, something raw that makes her gut tighten. Dark is a man with a lot of information and a high price. "I gave him everything, and he gave me you."

"You think we're here to save you?" she presses, voice low but coiled with menace. "You think we're your safety net? We're not here to babysit anyone."

Her words land like blows—hard and unforgiving. Niall recoils but scrambles forward anyway, desperation driving him closer. The wind howls around them now, carrying his voice up into the void as he shouts:

"Please! Y—You don't understand! I saw what they did—I *know things*! You have to protect me!"

Sloane laughs then—short and sharp and cruel as a knife blade glinting in firelight. "Protect you?" Her amusement is ice-cold. "What makes you think we care?"

"Because..." His voice catches—a rasp clawing its way out of his throat as terror chokes him. He looks over his shoulder like he expects shadows to peel away from the night and devour him whole.

"If you don't help me," he gasps finally, fear bleeding into every word, "I won't help you."

Ceige freezes.

"They have eyes everywhere," Niall spits out between ragged breaths. His shoulders shake under the weight of truths too big for someone this small to carry alone. "You have to be smarter than this."

The silence stretches thin as wire between them.

Ceige sees it then—etched across every line of his face: Fear so deep it razes him hollow from the inside out. Guilt anchoring him where he stands despite everything screaming at him to run. But there's something else hidden in those trembling blue eyes too—a spark he hasn't managed to kill yet.

A flicker of defiance.

It's fragile but alive.

"Talk," she says finally—her voice slicing through the moment with surgical precision. The single word lands heavy in the frost-laden air between them. "Now."

Shadows curl tighter around them as Niall shivers visibly, his breath hitching as he fights every instinct telling him not to speak.

"I know everything about Eira," he says at last—voice soft but steady enough for the weight of what comes next.

"Her experiments... the things she's done..." He swallows hard before finishing: "Things you wouldn't believe."

Behind her, Sloane shifts lazily—silent no longer but oozing mockery as she steps closer, boots crunching softly against frozen ground.

"Then let's not waste time." Her words cut sideways like a blade sliding between ribs—slow yet deliberate in their malice—and she gestures toward that precarious briefcase still dangling from Niall's trembling hand.

"What's in there?" A faint smirk curls at her lips—a tease sharpened by danger laced beneath it all. "Or are you just lugging around empty promises?"

The man falters but doesn't fall this time; somehow he finds footing enough in himself not to crumble completely.

"It's everything," Niall says at last—his breath visible now like smoke curling upward toward unseen gods watching overhead somewhere beyond Cryosium's skyless dome of ice-black nightfall stars gone dead long ago...

"This is what you need," Niall continues quietly until the wind screams.

A banshee wail tearing through the alley like icy claws.

Sloane's whistle cuts through it, sharp and shrill—a blade of sound that slices the chaos in two. Ceige hears it, feels it, before she even processes what it means. A signal.

A warning. Death closing in. The fire in her chest flares hot in the storm.

Her body moves before her mind catches up. Instinct takes over. Muscle and memory working as one. Her hand finds the familiar weight of steel at her hip, and the gun is out, steady in her grip. She pivots sharply, placing herself between Niall and the shadows creeping closer, swallowing the light with their menace.

"Down," she snaps, voice cutting through the gale like a whip crack. Niall doesn't move at first—his face frozen wide-eyed, fear locking his limbs in place as the figures emerge from the snow. They glide forward like phantoms, weapons glinting faintly in the pale gray light.

Here for blood.

Sloane's voice crawls out from somewhere in the dark behind them—a low mutter with a grin tucked into it. "Well," she says softly, "let's dance."

The first shot rips through the air.

Ceige fires back without hesitation, bullets tearing through snow-laden shadows. The crack of gunfire drowns out even the howling wind, each burst an answer to the death they've brought with them. One figure jerks as her shot lands true and crumples into the frost-bitten dirt, crimson spreading beneath him—warm blood meeting cold ground and steaming in defiance.

"Nice," Sloane calls out, her own weapon joining in with vicious barks that echo off ice-slicked walls. Each pull of her trigger is sharp and precise, each bullet an extension of her will. Another shadow falls, collapsing into itself like a marionette with its strings cut.

But there's no time to pause. No time to count bodies or bullets.

Ceige catches movement from the corner of her eye—a man breaking free from the shadows, desperation carved into every line of his face as he barrels toward her. Fast but reckless. He doesn't see her pivot until it's too late.

She takes a step forward, sidestepping his charge and letting his momentum carry him into nothingness. Her fist cracks against his jaw—bone meeting bone with a sickening crunch—and he staggers back just enough for her to raise her gun again and finish him cleanly. He drops wordlessly into the snow.

Sloane laughs.

The rhythm of violence pulls them both along now—a deadly duet honed by years of shared survival. Each action is automatic: aim and fire, dodge and strike. The alley reeks of blood and cordite as bodies fall one by one into the winter gloom.

No room for thought.

No time for mercy.

Bullets scream.

Shadows flail.

The cold bites harder than steel, but Ceige doesn't flinch. The alley is alive with chaos, and she moves through it like a storm given flesh.

"Idiots don't know when to quit," she mutters, words swallowed by the din. A bullet hisses past her ear, close enough to sting. She ducks low, her body moving before her mind catches up. Instinct. Survival.

A glance to her side—Niall. Frozen. Wide-eyed. He's a statue carved from fear, pale and trembling, waiting for death to find him.

"Move!" Ceige snaps, her voice cutting through the clamor like a blade. "Get behind cover!"

He doesn't respond at first, doesn't even blink. Just stands there, a skinny silhouette in the crosshairs of oblivion. She sees it happen before it happens—his blood pooling dark on snow, his body crumpling in a heap.

Stop it.

"Now!" she barks again, sharper this time, already turning back to the fight. No time to babysit cowards. Not here. Not tonight.

A yelp snaps her focus back to him—Niall scrambling toward a dumpster, panicked limbs jerking like some frantic marionette. He crouches low behind the rusted metal, half-hidden but still shaking so hard she can feel it from where she stands.

Pathetic.

But alive.

Ceige exhales hard through gritted teeth and squeezes the trigger. Her aim doesn't waver—never does—and another body drops in the alley ahead of her, folding lifeless into the shadows like paper set aflame. The air curdles with gunpowder and blood, sharp as winter itself.

"Three left!" Sloane's voice cuts through the carnage like laughter in a graveyard—dry and mocking, almost playful. "You good?"

Ceige doesn't answer with words—just a tight nod over her shoulder before sighting her next target. Determination carves itself into every line of her face like frost etching glass.

No room for doubt now.

Not ever.

She steps forward—not running, not hesitating—each movement sharp as a dagger's edge. They come at her like fools chasing ghosts, and she cuts them down just as easily. One by one they fall—slumped piles of flesh and failure against icy brick walls.

When silence finally takes hold of the alley, it feels louder than the gunfire ever was.

Ceige exhales slowly through parted lips as she surveys what remains—a tableau of broken bodies strewn across slick pavements, steam rising faintly where warm blood meets frozen ground.

The wind howls above it all.

Sloane strides up beside her with that insufferable smirk in place, brushing dust off her jacket like they've just finished some mundane chore instead of slaughtering Judex in Cryosium's frozen veins.

"Well," Sloane says lightly, tossing her words into the static-charged silence between them. "Wasn't that fun."

Ceige gives her a dry look but says nothing at first—just tugs off a glove and flexes stiff fingers against the cold night air. Her pulse still pounds in rhythm with every shallow breath pulled from ice-crisp air.

"Oh for the love of…you've been Trumped!" Sloane says as she points and laughs. Ceige raises a hand to her ear and feels an almost frozen trickle of blood. Barely there.

"Next time?" she deadpans finally without looking at Sloane, "Try being less dramatic."

Sloane snorts soft amusement but doesn't reply beyond an easy shrug—the kind only someone unbothered by proximity to death could manage—and Ceige turns instead toward Niall's quivering form behind the dumpster.

He's still crouched there—small and crumpled—and his head jerks up when Ceige steps closer like he expects to be struck down just for existing.

"You alive?" she asks flatly but not unkindly.

It takes him a moment too long to answer—a shaky nod followed by a stammered "Y-yeah… I'm fine." But neither his voice nor his eyes carry conviction strong enough to sell it; fear clings thick to every word he stutters out into frigid air.

"Good," she says, her voice sharp as the frost-coated air. Her gaze hardens. The streets of Cryosium don't forgive mistakes. And right now its streets are littered with them.

Ceige leads the way up the crumbling fire escape, each step a treacherous crunch on frost-slick metal. Behind her, Niall stumbles. His breath rasps in short, panicked gasps that rise like smoke in the frigid air. Fear radiates off him, raw and electric, buzzing through the silence. Ceige can feel it, humming against her nerves like static.

Something—someone—is off.

She glances back down into the alley—a dark vein carved through the skeletal city—expecting shadows to move within the swirling snow. None do. Just them then—a battered trio climbing toward salvation or death on a ladder of rust and ice.

The old fire escape is from a time when fire was stronger than snow and ice. Long gone.

"Move it, Niall!" she snaps without looking back. The wind whips at her face, stinging her skin raw, but adrenaline burns through her chest and pushes her forward. Every groan of metal under their weight feels like a clock ticking down. Time slipping away. Chances with it.

"I'm trying! I'm trying!" Niall wheezes, his voice thin with desperation as he fumbles for footing on the icy rungs. Ceige grits her teeth and rolls her eyes. This guy?

He's dead weight with a pulse—a liability wrapped around a secret.

The rooftop is a wasteland of white and gray stretching into forever beneath a gunmetal sky. The wind howls across it, tearing at their clothes and driving snow into their eyes. Ceige barely notices; she's scanning the empty expanse before them, instincts screaming like an alarm set too late.

Sloane breaks onto the roof seconds after—they always count in seconds here—and for a moment, she's nothing but chaos: wild hair whipping across her face, snow clinging to her jacket, boots crunching hard against ice-coated concrete. Her eyes blaze with something fierce and unbroken.

"Those fuckers were waiting for us," Sloane spits as she brushes snow off her sleeves, shaking off death like it's dust on her shoulder. Her words cut through the wind like glass shards—sharp edges of fury tempered by disbelief. "Eira's slipping."

"Or desperate," Ceige mutters without turning from where Niall has slumped against a rusted vent pipe. His chest heaves as he drags greedy gulps of air into his lungs; his limbs shake under some collapsing weight only he can feel.

"You good?" Ceige asks curtly.

"Y-yeah..." He doesn't sound good—he sounds broken—but what does that matter now? His trembling hands clutch the briefcase like it holds salvation itself—or damnation—and the sight sends something cold plunging into Ceige's gut.

"Your minute's up," Sloane snaps before he can catch another breath. Her words slice through him like steel through ice, leaving no room for softness or patience because there's none left between them anymore. "We've got bigger problems than your breakdown." She steps closer, eyes narrowing on him like rifle sights locking onto a target. "What do you know? Talk."

Niall flinches under their gaze—wide-eyed prey cornered by hunters—but he doesn't run because there's nowhere left to go except down into shadow or forward into fire.

"They were after me!" His voice cracks like brittle glass just before it shatters altogether, rising with frantic energy that feels too loud even here in this wasteland of endless wind and silence. "Eira knows I want to talk! She knows!" The words tumble out now—not spoken but spilled—rushed and chaotic as if trying to claw their way free before they're silenced forever. "I-I have proof! Evidence... everything they've done—the experiments—the horrors... It has to stop!"

Ceige crosses her arms and tilts her head slightly, letting his panic ricochet harmlessly off her stoic exterior while something colder twists deep inside her chest.

"Yeah?" she says flatly, voice colder than the air around them and twice as cutting. "And why should we protect you?"

For a second—less than that—her mask almost cracks; something flickers behind those hard eyes: empathy? Doubt? It vanishes almost as quickly as it appeared.

The only thing colder than this rooftop is trust—or the lack of it—and Ceige isn't ready to let hers thaw yet.

The wind screams, tearing across the rooftop, dragging sheets of snow like ghostly veils. Ceige braces against it, cold slicing through her as she squints into the storm. Below, Cryosium murmurs its relentless threat—distant sirens wail, a predator's growl carried on the icy air.

Her heart beats hard against her ribs, still pounding from the ambush. But it's not just the fight that twists her gut into knots. It's Niall. The man is a ruin—shaking hands clutching at the edges of his coat, eyes darting to shadows that don't yet exist. A wreck clinging to fraying threads of desperation.

"Please," he gasps, his breath fogging and dissipating into the frozen ether. He stumbles closer, knees threatening to buckle. "You have to help me. If they find out I'm here—if they know I've talked—"

"They'll kill you." Sloane cuts him off like a blade hitting bone, taking a step forward, her wild curls whipping in the wind. Her voice seethes with impatience, green eyes narrowing on him. "Newsflash—you're not special. We're not exactly untouchable here ourselves."

"And worst of all, you aren't talking," Sloane says.

Niall flinches like she slapped him. His head jerks toward the edges of the roof again, as if he expects shadows to materialize from the snow and drag him under.

"You need me!" he cries suddenly, his voice cracking in the bitter air. "I'm your only chance to take Eiskorp down! Please—I can't go back!" His words tumble out in frantic bursts now, spilling over each other with every ragged breath. "She'll kill me if she knows I'm here... but I can't die without telling the truth."

"Truth means shit if you're dead," Ceige snaps, anger rising unbidden like heat against the cold. Reality presses heavy against her shoulders, an unrelenting thing that bites deeper than ice. Her gaze flicks to Sloane's—a silent exchange passed between them in the storm: a spark of shared resolve wrapped in jagged doubt.

Sloane exhales sharply and crosses her arms against the cold. "We aren't your babysitters," she says finally, words cutting clean through Niall's babble. "We're your lifeline. You want to live? Start talking straight and give us what we need."

Niall opens his mouth but falters—and Ceige doesn't miss how his hands tremble harder now than before. Whether it's from fear or cold or both doesn't matter;

what matters is that those hands hold something sharp enough to cut them all open.

"I'll tell you everything," he whispers at last—not strong or steady or brave but broken and small. "At my place. 7A Dempster U. It's there. The briefcase is a ploy."

Ceige feels her instincts scream louder than Cryosium's winds: *This is wrong.* But she presses it down deep where she buries most things these days.

A broken dam bursts.

Desperation floods out.

"I can help you!" Niall's voice trembles, cracking under the weight of fear. "Eira's experiments—they're worse than anything you've imagined. I know things… horrible things. I can show you!"

Ceige cuts him off like a blade slicing through frost. "Lead on." Her words are as sharp as the ice beneath their feet. She studies him in the cold, her gaze peeling back flesh and bone, searching for the truth buried beneath his panic. But all she finds is fear, raw and ripe, tangled with guilt. It clings to him like a second skin.

The wind howls around them, gnashing its teeth against her resolve. Ceige leans close to Sloane and murmurs, her voice nearly lost to the storm. "Someone hired me to kill Eira," she says. The words feel heavy and bitter, a confession dragged out by the icy gale. "But I didn't sign up to play bodyguard for a guy who might be a liability."

Sloane doesn't miss a beat. Her sharp laugh cuts through the night, dry and sardonic. "Torn between your morals and survival again?" Her grin is razor-thin, curling with knowing contempt. "Classic Ceige. We don't have time for this crap. Decide—are we lugging this guy along or throwing him to the wolves?"

Ceige's eyes narrow, her breath coiling in front of her face like smoke. "Sweetheart," she says, low and lethal, "I don't throw people to wolves. I shoot them."

It's bravado—an armor too easy to slip into—but doubt stirs in the pit of her stomach like something alive and writhing. Niall could be chaos waiting to strike. Or maybe he really is just some pitiful creature, cornered, shaking, too blind to see past his own terror.

"I—" Niall lurches forward, but Sloane snaps out an arm like a whip to stop him cold.

"Shut it!" Her bark cuts through his pleas with brutal precision; her patience dangles by a single thread stretched too thin across too many hours of tension. "No more promises, no more bullshit! Don't move."

Her fingers glide over her comm device—a quick flick of delicate precision for someone so outwardly rough-edged—activating the scanner strapped to her wrist. The air gnaws at her skin in savage bites of cold; winter doesn't care about waiting games or moral quandaries.

"Hold still," Sloane growls under her breath without looking at him directly, focusing instead on the scan's readout as it flickers across her screen with sterile indifference. "I'm not interested in adding 'murderer' to my résumé tonight."

Niall shivers under her scrutiny—the cornered animal again—eyes darting wildly as if escape lies somewhere just beyond his reach. "I—I swear I'm not armed!" he stammers, trembling like he expects frostbite or bullets at any second.

Sloane doesn't answer immediately; she waits for the scan's reply instead.

Beep.

"Clean," it says.

For now.

Sloane steps back without lowering her guard and gives him one last hard look—a gaze built from iron bars that smash through pretense and panic alike. "You better stay that way," she mutters darkly, "or next time you're going back to Eira in pieces."

The threat hangs in the air like frozen breath—sharp-edged, shimmering with finality—and then she turns away from him altogether.

Ceige already has her eyes on the rooftop's edge when Sloane falls silent beside her. The horizon stretches out ahead of them—a pale sheet smeared with streaks of gray—and snowflakes spiral down slow and soundless around their boots as if trying to smother every trace of life left behind.

"No more delays," Ceige says quietly but firmly as she surveys what little path remains visible through the curtains of white that seem intent on swallowing them whole.

Not far enough ahead yet—

Not nearly safe enough yet—

Snow deadens sound but never intention; they both know someone—or something—is out there watching still.

Waiting still.

And so they move forward anyway because there isn't any other choice.

Sloane doesn't look back this time. Doesn't need to. Her voice alone is enough to command obedience. Ice masks her face, but there's steel beneath it—a quiet determination veiled by her usual bravado. "Don't trip," she says, a blade hidden in silk.

Niall stumbles behind them, his steps unsteady, his breath quick and shallow. He's a flickering light in the gale, fragile but still burning, and he carries the weight of everything. Their mission. Their chance. Their survival. Cryosium's dirtiest secrets rest with him, yet he looks like he might shatter at any second—a snowflake pressed too hard between fingers. They can't lose him. Can't let him fall apart now.

Sloane moves ahead, cutting through the storm like a wraith. She doesn't hesitate, doesn't falter as she leaps from one frozen rooftop to the next, her body tight with precision, every movement honed to perfection. A shadow gliding through chaos. "Babysitting a whistleblower in this shitstorm," she mutters under her breath, curls whipping wild across her face like the lashing winds. "What a goddamn mess."

"Better than being dead," Ceige throws back, her words flat and cold as the snow building on their shoulders. She doesn't look at Sloane, doesn't break her focus on the churning storm ahead—the sirens screaming somewhere in its depths like wolves baying for blood. "Eyes forward."

"Sure," Sloane snaps back with a razor-sharp grin that cuts through the frost. "Because nothing says 'safe' like rooftops sheathed in ice." But even as she spits sarcasm into the howling wind, her heart drums its own rhythm—quick, erratic, alive. This is why she does it: for the thrill that presses sharp against her ribs, for the electric jolt of danger threading through her veins.

The wind howls louder as they reach another gap—wider this time, more treacherous—and Niall falters mid-leap.

One foot slips on ice; gravity pulls hard at his frame like invisible claws scraping him toward the abyss below—black and endless and waiting to swallow him whole.

"Careful!" Ceige barks sharply as her hand shoots out instinctively to grab his arm before he disappears into nothingness. Her grip is firm and steady; it anchors him when all else feels like it's unraveling into chaos around them. The warmth of her hand barely registers against the cold eating away at their flesh—but Niall nods weakly, gratitude shining dimly through eyes clouded with fear.

As they slip further into the storm, the weight of their mission settles heavily on Sloane's shoulders. Niall may be their ticket to exposing Eiskorp, but with every heartbeat echoing in the blizzard, Ceige knows the real battle has just begun. Behind them, the howling wind swallows their tracks, leaving only the quiet of falling snow—the calm before the storm.

Chapter 7

Ceige's boots strike the concrete.

Cold against colder.

Each step echoes, a hollow drumbeat swallowed by the icy dark. The tunnels twist beneath Cryosium like veins carved into the frozen skin of the world, jagged shadows bleeding secrets. The air bites—sharp as splinters of glass—and the snow above presses down, heavy and suffocating, a grave waiting to collapse. Each step is a fight against it. No room for hesitation. Not here.

"Did you hear me? Eiskorp's going to pay!" Niall blurts out, his voice thin, unraveling into the void. It breaks the silence but leaves it hungrier. He flits between Ceige and Sloane, his wide eyes darting to every corner of the shadowed labyrinth like some unseen hand might snatch him back into whatever hell spat him out. "I—I'll tell them everything! The court! The UN! Anyone who'll listen!"

Sloane laughs—a low growl curling through the cold. "Sure you will," she says, her grin flashing quick and sharp beneath the tangle of black curls that frame her face like wildfire. She moves like a predator, each step deliberate, her heat radiating in waves that don't belong in this frozen tomb. A living blaze beside Ceige's frozen edge.

"Not funny!" Niall snaps, scurrying forward like he can outrun her mockery—or the tension trailing them all. It clings close, thick as smoke and just as stifling. Ceige glances back at him, watching his panic spark between them like static electricity in the frost-heavy air. His jacket hangs loose on his thin frame, frayed edges whispering of another life—a warmer life he barely remembers now. But here? Here they're just ghosts slipping through catacombs built on failures and betrayals long gone cold.

They stop at a corner where light gives way to dying embers—a flicker before oblivion swallows it whole. Niall hesitates there, breath catching as he crouches to shift aside a rotting board wedged tight against the wall. Wood groans beneath his trembling hands before it gives way with a hollow sigh, revealing an open maw beneath it—a black hole yawning wide with ancient hunger.

"This is it," he breathes.

Ceige steps forward without hesitation, her voice cold enough to freeze midair: "Lead on."

Her eyes flick sideways as Sloane's silhouette slides up beside her—silent but challenging every step of the way. They move together into the waiting void where mildew drips down walls slick with rust and shadows press closer like unseen hands clawing at their throats. The stink rises to meet them—thick and wet with rot—clinging to their skin until breathing feels like swallowing decay itself.

"Just wait," Niall whispers again from ahead, his voice trembling on a tightrope between awe and dread. "Just wait until you see what I've got."

Ceige doesn't answer. She watches the shadows instead.

They twist. They writhe.

Like vipers in a pit. Like memories clawing out of graves she'd long thought sealed.

The tunnel narrows around them, walls pressing like ribs against lungs that can't draw enough air. Their steps drag heavier now, weighted by something unseen—something waiting ahead, or stalking behind. Ceige can't tell anymore which direction holds more danger.

But there's no going back. Not when each breath reeks of inevitability.

"Don't get too cozy," Sloane says, her voice slicing through the damp and decay like a razor through skin. "This isn't a sightseeing trip."

Her fingers twitch near her hip, betraying nerves her tone refuses to concede. She's ready to move, ready to fight, but not steady enough to mask the fracture beneath her composure. That same tension coils in Ceige's chest—a restless fire that flares hotter with every step deeper into this grave of truths they should have left buried.

"Not sightseeing," Niall mutters as he shuffles past, his words jittery and uneven, his body radiating panic like heat from scorched earth. "I just—I need to find it." He falls to his knees at the edge of a jagged hole, hands clawing desperately at the frozen debris like an animal digging for escape from a collapsing burrow. Rocks skitter across the icy floor as Ceige braces herself for the ceiling to come down on top of them, entombing them in frost and ruin.

But it doesn't fall.

Instead, with a sharp gasp, Niall pries something loose from the wreckage—a small, battered thing he clutches against his chest as if it might keep him from shattering completely.

"Let me see," Ceige says, her voice cracking across his panic like a whip.

The air thickens, stretching taut like an overstretched wire ready to snap. Niall's breaths come ragged and uneven; his eyes dart between them and the object in his hands as though weighing its worth against their looming judgment. The shadows shift and ripple across the frostbitten walls, creeping ever closer—silent spectators to whatever truth is about to crawl out into the light.

Ceige feels it then—the weight of what comes next pressing hard against her ribs. They're balanced on a razor's edge now, one tremor away from going over into oblivion.

Niall takes a step deeper into his so-called sanctuary—a place that barely deserves the name. Acid-green light leaks from sputtering chemical lamps above their heads, staining everything it touches in sickly hues of decay. The warmth is sucked from the air; frost crusts along cracked metal panels and bites at exposed skin.

Papers. Rusted machines. Towers of obsolete tech stacked high and precarious in every corner of this suffocating crypt masquerading as salvation.

Niall drags himself toward his frost-rimmed desk, setting down a battered briefcase with hands trembling as if caught in an unrelenting arctic windstorm. The locks snap open—sharp clicks breaking the brittle silence like gunfire echoing in narrow canyons.

He lied about it being a ploy.

Ceige doesn't answer him. Her eyes trace the shadows instead—shadows that shift and slither like memories she thought she'd buried long ago but feel dangerously alive down here.

The tunnel tightens around them as they press on, steps falling heavier now under the weight of what lies ahead—or behind; Ceige doesn't know anymore which direction feels more dangerous. But there's no turning back now—not when each breath tastes of inevitability.

"Don't get too comfortable down here," Sloane quips, her sarcasm cutting through layers of mildew and dread like glass scraping steel. "We're not sightseeing."

But Ceige notices how Sloane's fingers twitch near her side—ready for action but not quite composed enough to hide the crack in her armor. That fire burns hot in Sloane too—that same restless flame twisting inside Ceige's chest with every step deeper they take into this graveyard of secrets.

"Not sighseeing. Right, right," Niall stammers, shuffling past them with the jittery energy of a man unraveling. "I just—I need to find it." His fingers claw at the jagged edge of the hole like a drowning man scrabbling for a lifeline, sending loose debris scattering across the frozen floor. For a moment, Ceige braces for the whole structure to collapse, burying them in a tomb of ice and ruin. But then, with a sharp intake of breath, Niall drags the ice-covered door open, clutching it against his chest as though it might anchor him to sanity.

"Let's see this place," Ceige orders, her voice sharp enough to cut through his panic.

The air grows taut, suspended in a tenuous balance between revelation and disaster. Ceige watches Niall wrestle himself into focus, his breathing ragged as he prepares to unveil whatever salvation—or damnation—he's been hiding. Shadows crawl along the frostbitten walls, silent witnesses to truths better left buried. Ceige feels the weight of the moment press against her ribs: they are perched on a hazardous ledge, one misstep away from plunging into oblivion.

Niall's so-called sanctuary is bathed in an acidic green glow that leeches warmth from the air. The chemical lights sputter faintly, casting warped shadows over the haphazard towers of papers and obsolete tech crowding every surface. The space is suffocating—a crypt masquerading as refuge. Niall moves to his frost-rimmed desk, setting down his battered briefcase with hands that tremble as if caught in an arctic gale. The metal locks snap open with sharp clicks that ricochet off the narrow walls like distant gunfire.

"This," Niall breathes, snapping the battered case open with trembling hands, "this is what I've been working on." The words leave him like vapor—thin, fragile, barely clinging to form. He pulls out a laptop, its edges dented and screen cracked, the machine sparking to life with a flicker that jitters before vomiting images and text across the glass. Files spill out in chaotic waves—broken fragments, disjointed phrases—like ghosts clawing at the surface of a too-thin veil.

Ceige leans in, her eyes narrowing as she sifts through the debris onscreen. Shreds of documents overlain with frantic scrawls. Scribbled notes that bleed into senseless noise. Her scarred brow tightens; her mouth presses into a thin line. "A rabbit hole," she whispers, her voice sharp and taut—a blade dulled by disappointment. She'd hoped for clarity that would cut deep into Eiskorps' armor. Instead, she sees madness. Obsession spiraling into futility.

"Wait!" Niall's voice cracks as he lunges at the screen, stabbing at it with one trembling finger. "Just wait! Listen to me! They're hunting me—they've already found me!" His words rush out like floodwater breaching a dam, spilling everywhere uncontrollably. "I saw them last night—outside my safe house! They... they were there!"

Sloane shifts in the corner, unfolds her arms from across her chest. Steps forward slow and deliberate, coiled muscle in liquid motion. Her lips curl into something like a sneer but colder—something venomous enough to burn frost into flesh. "Is that so?" she drawls, voice dripping disdain. Her gaze fixes on him like a steel trap snapping shut—merciless and final. "Then tell me how you managed to slip past Judex last night and yet land here today with them at your heels."

Niall flinches under the weight of her words but pushes back with stammered defiance. "Because... because I know things!" His voice pitches higher as his bravado unravels like rotten cloth tearing away from metal bones. He grips the laptop tighter as if it might anchor him somehow or shield him from their judgments. "I have evidence," he gasps—his desperation bleeding through every syllable now. "Real evidence! They think I'm nothing—but I've seen things, things they'd kill anyone to keep buried!"

Ceige doesn't move at first; she only watches him through cold eyes sharp as fractured ice. Then she steps closer—slowly, deliberately—and lets her shadow fall over him like dusk swallowing daylight whole. When she speaks, it comes low and even, each word cutting clean: "Do you have evidence?"

The question severs his frenzy mid-breath.

"Shut up!" he snaps suddenly, the raw edge in his voice slicing into the room like jagged glass spat from a collapsing windowpane. His head jerks toward the darkness beyond them; his eyes flicker wildly through their dim surroundings as if he can already see death stalking just beyond reach. His fear spills out unchecked now: "You don't get it—they're everywhere! Watching us... waiting... closing in! There!"

"Turn around," Sloane whispers—a hiss softer than falling ash but no less lethal. Her hand drops to her weapon with an ease born of repetition; Ceige mirrors her instinctually, fingers curling tight against cold steel grips.

The air itself seems to freeze.

Shadows stretch long across the walls—alive and shivering at their edges—as movement stirs within them just enough to feel wrong.

Just shadows.

Black phantoms in the dim air.

"That's all they are," Ceige murmurs, the words brittle as glass. A charm against the dark. Meant for Sloane, but just as much for herself. She keeps her eyes fixed on Niall. He curls over his laptop like a man shielding himself from a gale, sweat slicking his brow despite the chill. It isn't the cold making him tremble. The frost clinging to him isn't ice—it's guilt.

"All right, genius," she says, her voice cutting low. Sharp. Hard as flint. "Show us this so-called evidence. Now. No more theatrics."

"Just—just give me a second!" Niall barks back, fingers hammering at the keys. Erratic, frantic. His hands jitter like they've been pulled loose from their moorings, each keystroke striking notes of panic in the suffocating quiet. Seconds vanish into the bitter air, unnoticed but unbearable.

"Tick-tock." Sloane's voice, flat and quiet, slices through the tension like a razor gliding just beneath skin. Her hand flexes at her side, restless. Desperate to move, to fight, to *do*. The walls inch closer—or maybe it's just her imagination—but the cold is real enough, gnawing its way through skin and bone like teeth of broken ice.

"There!" Niall shouts suddenly, spinning the laptop around with hands that shake more than steady it. Wild eyes search theirs for some spark of understanding—but the screen stares them down with mocking indifference. Distorted pixels smear into jagged shapes and static hums like dead air between radio stations. A maze of digital ruin collapsing in on itself.

Ceige's mouth twists—not quite a smile but something darker—as she folds her arms tightly over her chest. "Wow," she says flatly, each word dripping acid. "Pretty convincing stuff—you've got me right on the edge of my seat."

"No!" Niall's voice cracks open like glass dropped from a height. Shattered syllables spilling out as he jabs wildly at the keyboard again and again and again. "It's here! I swear it's here! Just give me—"

Ceige leans forward, stepping toward the screen without breaking her gaze from that unrelenting void creeping in at the edges of her sightline—a shadow tide rising just out of view. The laptop flickers once—twice—and then locks into place.

Cruel clarity.

Words march across the screen in perfect precision: *Humanity is an outdated protocol.* Again and again they scroll past—a hollow mantra stripped bare of meaning or mercy—until they blur into something nauseatingly rhythmic.

Mechanical hymns for a godless machine.

Humanity is an outdated protocol. Humanity is an outdated protocol. Humanity is an outdated protocol. Humanity is an outdated protocol. Humanity is an outdated protocol. Humanity is an outdated protocol. Humanity is an outdated protocol. Humanity is an outdated protocol. Humanity is an outdated protocol. Humanity is an outdated protocol. Humanity is an outdated protocol. Humanity is an outdated protocol. Humanity is an outdated protocol. Humanity is an outdated protocol. Humanity is an outdated protocol. Humanity is an outdated protocol. Humanity is...

Ceige presses her fingers to the bridge of her nose. A low groan escapes her throat, raw and guttural. "This?" she says, words sharp as shattered glass. "This is what we're risking our necks for? A glitching ghost of a bad sci-fi dream?"

Sloane leans in, close enough that Ceige can feel her gaze more than see it. Her green eyes narrow—not at the screen but at Ceige's face. The flickering light from the monitor carves deep shadows across Sloane's features: gold catching in the wild arcs of her curls, darkness pooling beneath the high planes of her cheekbones. She looks otherworldly—like something pulled out of fire and ash, a wisp caught between fever dreams and nightmares.

"It's a setup," Ceige spits suddenly. The words crack like gunfire, heat flaring up beneath layers of taut frustration and something darker—something colder. Her hand falls from her face, slicing through the air toward nothing in particular but everything at once—everything this moment has become. "But not us. Not senior Judex. Back there? Playing hero with their shiny little tricks?" She laughs bitterly, a hollow sound that doesn't quite echo. "Amateurs. The attackers are juniors, beginners."

"Were. They *were* juniors. Now they are dead." Sloane snaps back before Ceige can continue. There's an edge to her tone, hard as flint but splintered with confusion. Her hand twitches at her side—a reflex caught between thought and memory. The skirmish is still fresh on her skin: adrenaline coiled tight in muscle and bone like it hasn't quite let go yet. "But they were armed, Ceige. Armed and trying to kill us."

"No." Ceige turns sharply on her heel, pacing now, each step jagged against the cold expanse of the room's metal floor. The hum of machinery presses against them—constant, guttural, oppressive. "They weren't here for us," she says tightly, voice all edges now. "Those Judex came for Niall." The name drops like lead into silence before she continues: "He's not just some witness hiding out there—he's a weapon gone rogue."

"I am not!" Niall's voice cracks, sharp and jagged, like ice splintering underfoot. His blue eyes cut between them, frantic, desperate. Desperation coils around him, tight and suffocating, stinking of fear. "I've seen things! You have to believe me!"

"Believe what?" Ceige spins on him, her movement a whip slicing through brittle air. Her finger stabs the laptop screen where the words scroll endlessly, hollow as a corpse: ***Humanity is an outdated protocol.*** "That? You're spitting static. Look at yourself. You've been rewired."

"But he knows things," Sloane says softly, her voice thin as frost on a windowpane. Empathy dulls the edge of her defiance, softening her in ways she wishes it wouldn't. "What if... what if we could use him?"

"Use him?" Ceige's words are flint against steel—sharp sparks in the cold. Her voice drops into a low grind, deliberate and cutting. "Use him for what? To throw to the wolves?" Her gaze locks onto Sloane's, hard and unyielding as winter stone. "This isn't a game, Sloane. It's not some storybook rescue. We don't save people who are already drowning in Eiskorps' tide." She steps closer; her words are knives now. "You know what happens when you trust the wrong person."

Sloane stiffens but doesn't step back. Her chin lifts—a small rebellion—but her voice wavers just enough to betray what she'd rather not admit. "So... what do we do?"

"It's simple." Ceige exhales, slow and measured, her breath curling in frozen tendrils before vanishing into the void. "We walk away." Her voice hardens into iron—final and unrelenting. "He's not worth the risk."

"You're playing with fire," Sloane whispers, urgency clinging to the edges of her words like frost melting under faint sunlight.

"Better than letting it burn us alive." Ceige turns sharply on her heel and strides toward the exit without looking back; shadows spill behind her like ink dragged by an unseen hand. Her parting words fall heavy in the air: cold and unyielding. "Stay close."

The tunnels swallow them whole.

An abyss of black stretches endlessly ahead—and presses relentlessly from all sides. The walls shift with each step they take; jagged edges loom like old wounds left to fester in darkness and ice. Behind them, Niall's voice lingers—a ghost caught in the frozen air: ***"Humanity is an outdated protocol!"*** The phrase bounces off walls slick with frost and echoes until it bleeds into silence.

But silence doesn't erase it.

The words carve themselves deep, embedding like hooks beneath skin—impossible to dislodge.

The labyrinth tightens around them; every step is heavier now, every breath thinner in this icy graveyard of forgotten things. Frost crunches beneath their boots—sharp cracks that ricochet through Ceige's raw nerves. The cold doesn't just bite—it sinks inward, filling spaces she tries to keep sealed off inside herself.

"Did you see his face?" Sloane breaks the quiet, her words barely more than breath slipping through trembling lips. Her gaze scans the shadows that pool along the edges of their path as if something might rise up from within them. "He looked like he was already dead."

"Good," Ceige says. The word is steel, cold and blunt. She doesn't slow. "Death suits him."

The air cleaves at the sound, her voice slicing sharp and clean—but inside, there's a shift, faint but certain. A crack through iron: doubt, faint as breath against glass. She buries it deeper.

Sloane laughs—a short, brittle sound that snaps like dry twigs underfoot. "Careful," she says. Her tone drips with something between sarcasm and warning. "Keep prodding the fire, and you'll burn too."

Ahead, the path splits—a fork yawning open into twin voids. Shadow swallows stone walls slick as oil; faint light from aboveground pipes glimmers weakly before dying in the black. What waits beyond—safety or ruin—remains unspoken.

"North Underground's straight ahead," Ceige mutters. The words are clipped, measured. Like speaking them might turn them solid, give them weight to push forward one more step. It isn't hope she clings to—it's a destination carved into her mind like a brand: respite, weapons, survival. They'll find it in North Underground.

They have to.

Sloane hesitates as they reach the crossroads. Her gaze lingers over one shoulder, back toward what they've left behind—the fragile walls of sanctuary now fading into memory.

"Do you think he'll make it?" she asks quietly.

Ceige stops. Not long enough to seem uncertain, but long enough for irritation to curl tight in her throat and press against her teeth. "Who cares?" The words drop like stones into a frozen pond: heavy and flat. "It doesn't matter."

Her jaw sets hard; her tone sharpens like cracked ice underfoot. "We have a mission. I have a mission."

Sloane's lips twist into something bitter and broken at the edges—a grimace more than a smile. "Some mission," she says softly, each syllable soaked in venomous disbelief. "What about the ones we leave behind?"

Ceige doesn't look back—not at Sloane, not at what her words cut open between them.

"Not everyone can be saved." Her voice is hard-edged this time—too sharp to bend—but her pulse betrays her again, slamming wild against her ribs like a trapped bird's wings beating uselessly at its cage. "Focus," she orders through clenched teeth. "We get out alive. We expose Eiskorp. Kill Eira." Each phrase carves itself into the cold air between them like tombstone inscriptions—final and unyielding. "That's how we help anyone."

Sloane exhales slowly; the sound fades before it even fully escapes her lips.

"Right. That's how I help Cass." Her answer is soft enough to disappear entirely under the weight of their silence. Doubt shivers across her expression—alive but fragile—as if caught in its death throes.

"What'd you say?" Ceige said. Her way of admitting she was not listening.

"I said you're an asshole," Sloane sneered.

Ceige moves again without waiting for anything more; boots crunch against ice-crusted ground with every step—a stark rhythm of survival in an unforgiving world where every breath feels borrowed.

The wind cuts at her face like razors—searing and sharp—but even that is muted beneath another weight pressing down on her mind like chains: Niall's words, cold iron wrapped around sinking thoughts that drag ever lower.

She glances sideways toward Sloane—the other woman's hair whipping wild against the bitter wind like defiance made manifest—and says nothing.

Between them lies only silence now: thick as frost on the stone around them, suffocating as black water rising too fast to swim clear of its pull.

Sloane cracks the silence.

Not gently. Impatient, like snapping frostbitten branches under her boots. "Is it always this dead down here?"

"No." Ceige keeps moving. Her eyes sweep through shadows that stretch between Cryosium's ruins—splintered skeletons clawing up from the frozen ground, carcasses left to wither in the open. Monuments to lives forgotten. Dreams buried beneath frost. "Quiet means one of two things. Waiting... or a trap."

Sloane huffs a laugh, dry and sharp as ice breaking underfoot. She drives her boot into an iced-over puddle, shards skittering like glass daggers across the snow. "I'll take thunder over whatever the hell that was back there."

"Focus." Ceige doesn't look at her. The word cuts clean, sharp—steel disguised as sound.

The alley rises ahead.

Narrow. Unmarked. Alive with menace. Darkness shifts here—not just absence of light, but something sentient, something waiting. A snare disguised as shadow, drawing them in with every step closer. It hums low, a siren's call stitched into the cold air.

Ceige stops at its mouth.

Hesitates—not long, but enough for doubt to creep in, icy fingers brushing the back of her neck. Retreat whispers soft promises—safety in solitude—but it's drowned out by something louder now: Sloane standing beside her, reckless and sure, radiating heat in this wasteland of ice and ash. Alone feels safer. Together feels fatal.

But Ceige moves anyway.

Not willingly.

Inevitably.

And steps into the cold waiting beyond.

Chapter 8

The North Underground breathes.

A pulse beneath the frostbitten corpse of the world above.

Hazy neon signs sputter and flicker, their light seeping through curtains of smoke, carving jagged halos onto walls that crumble like old parchment. The air hums—half electricity, half voices—laughter clashing with anger, whispers tangling with shouts. Shadows coil and stretch across faces, strangers and ghosts alike, while the stench of spilled whiskey and stale cigarettes clings to Ceige's skin like grease.

"Try to keep up, darling."

Sloane's voice slices through the din. Sharp. Careless. Her curls bob with each step as she glides through the crowd, carving a path like a blade through flesh. She moves as though the Underground bends to her, as though it belongs to her—or maybe, Ceige thinks, she belongs to it. She doesn't look back. She doesn't need to.

Ceige follows. Close but cautious. One hand brushing her side where pain still blooms from earlier in the night—an ache that beats in time with her pulse, a reminder of how close they were to losing. Everything.

Her eyes dart across the room, scanning faces, hands, movements too quick or too slow. Someone shifts in the corner; a coat gleams with something metallic as it catches fractured neon light. Heat rolls off bodies pressed too tightly together; sweat and smoke mix in the air until it's hard to breathe.

This place will burn, Ceige thinks.

A spark is all it'll take.

"Yeah," she mutters under her breath, "I'm keeping up." Her shoulder cuts into someone else's with enough force to earn a glare she ignores. She matches Sloane's pace but keeps her distance, her focus spread thin between the now and what waits ahead.

The booth sits at the edge of everything—the edge of shadows and noise and danger—a hollow little space tucked into the farthest corner where light barely touches.

Strategic.

Quiet.

Safe? No. Nowhere here is safe.

Ceige slides into the leather seat stiffly, her body tense despite herself. Muscles coiled tight beneath a disguise of practiced calm—relaxed limbs that lie about what lies beneath.

"Drink?" Sloane asks over her shoulder without waiting for an answer. Her voice lilts upward like she's asking for nothing at all, casual as air—but Ceige catches the steel hidden there beneath the surface grin. Knows better than most exactly how sharp Sloane can be when it suits her.

"Something strong," Ceige says flatly, exhaustion dulling her voice until it sounds almost detached. But not quite.

The tension between them lingers—the kind that doesn't shatter but stretches taut like wire ready to snap. A remnant of words unsaid and wounds unhealed stitched together by silence they both refuse to break.

For now.

The drinks land on the table.

Ceige drinks.

The burn scalds its way down, leaving embers in its wake. Heat feels wrong here—in a world shaped by ice, carved by survival. She exhales slow, steady. Finally lets herself look at Sloane.

Green eyes—emerald and wicked. Lips curved in a sly almost-smile, always on the verge of something: laughter, danger, both. Sloane is motion itself—chaos wrapped in wildfire. Ceige feels like stone beside her. Ice brushing fire.

When the drinks arrive, Ceige knocks back a mouthful without hesitation. The alcohol burns its way down her throat, leaving behind heat that feels out of place in a world built on ice and survival. She exhales slowly and finally lets herself study Sloane more closely—the vibrant green eyes now clouded with something darker than mischief, the tight set of lips that hint at a story never fully told.

"So?" Sloane leans closer now, voice dropping low enough so only Ceige can hear. Her words carry an edge sharper than any blade. "What's next?"

Her movements remain fluid, but there's a tension beneath the surface—a coiled energy that speaks of something more than just the mission. Ceige recognizes the look: a hunter's patience, a predator's focus.

"In and out," Ceige replies tersely. "Kill Eira and get gone. Cut off the head, see if the serpent dies." She forces herself to sound steady, knowing Sloane's motivations run deeper than a simple assignment. Sloane isn't assigned, she isn't getting paid.

Sloane's laugh is brief, more a bark than genuine humor. "Simple," she says, her voice tight. For a moment, something almost feral flashes in her eyes—a glimpse of a wound that never fully healed.

"You have history," Ceige states. It's not a question.

Sloane's smile turns razor-sharp. "Some people," she says slowly, each word measured, "deserve exactly what's coming to them." Her fingers curl around her glass, knuckles going white for just a moment before she relaxes.

"Noted," Ceige replies, understanding that some stories are never meant to be fully told.

Sloane leans back, her gaze sweeping the room, but Ceige can see the barely contained fury swimming just beneath her composure. Whatever drove Sloane to this moment was personal—a debt that could only be paid in blood.

"Fun times," Sloane says, her voice low and dangerous.

Ceige's gaze cools instantly—whatever softness had threatened breaks apart under frostbite edges once more.

Her voice becomes steel: calm as snow-choked wind slicing through dead trees outside.

"All according to plan."

The bar hums around them, a low, throaty growl of laughter and clinking glasses swallowed by shadows. Sloane raises her drink in a slow mock toast, the amber liquid catching the dim light like a dying star. "A plan? That's your idea of fun?" Her grin cuts across her face, sharp as a blade. Her eyes flash—dangerous, daring. "Fine. But when Eira's finished with us, you owe me a night worth remembering."

Ceige exhales a dry laugh, brittle as frost crunching underfoot. "Aren't we already in one?" Her words scrape the air between them, but the corners of her mouth betray something softer—a flicker of warmth fighting to survive the cold.

Sloane's grin widens, splitting her face like ice cracking under pressure. "Now you're getting it." She winks—brief as a spark—but there's weight beneath it, an unspoken oath forged in fire and tempered in ice: whatever waits ahead, they will take it on together.

The noise around them folds into itself, fading to a distant whisper. The static of voices blurs; the chiming of glasses dissolves into faint echoes. For that moment, it's just them—two women scarred by battles past and tethered by promises unspoken. Across from each other, they sit like sentinels bracing against the storm, preparing to descend into Eiskorp's frozen maw.

Ceige moves—deft and deliberate—slipping an old napkin from beneath Sloane's half-empty glass without spilling a drop. Around them, laughter swells and breaks like icy waves against jagged cliffs before fading back into nothingness. Ceige barely notices. Her focus sharpens to a point as she pulls an X-9 pen from her jacket pocket—a slender weapon in its own right—and clicks it once. The sound is precise, metallic, final.

Ink glistens at the tip.

"This isn't for fun," Ceige mutters under her breath. Her hand hovers over the napkin like a predator stalking its prey before pouncing. The pen presses down and begins to move—each stroke purposeful yet urgent. Lines slash across the fragile surface like the first cuts into virgin snow; circles bloom like frost patterns on glass; arrows spear their way toward unseen thresholds where hesitation equates to death.

Every mark isn't just a plan—it's a lifeline stretched taut over nothingness.

Sloane watches her work, her smirk curling upward like smoke rising from kindling just caught flame. "You're starting to scare me," she says with mock ease, though there's something edged beneath her voice. "Ink and paper? What are you going to do next? Tap out Morse code?"

"Quiet." Ceige doesn't look up—her voice flat but razor-sharp. "I'm thinking."

"Your 'genius' had better be good," Sloane murmurs with dark amusement as she leans closer. Her hand brush Ceige's—a fleeting touch warm enough to jolt but not quite melt through the cold closing in around them both. "Because we can't just stroll into Eira's penthouse and yell 'boo.'"

Ceige pauses for half a heartbeat before speaking again, her tone clipped as if every word costs too much to waste: "Elevator shaft."

Sloane raises an eyebrow—a challenge without words—but waits for more.

"Direct access." Ceige presses harder on the napkin now; the ink bleeds darker into fibers threatening to fray under pressure. "It's risky but fast." A pause hangs between them like frost suspended midair before shattering: "And only one stop."

"Hers."

"Or we take the maintenance shaft," Sloane says, her grin razor-sharp, eyes flickering with menace. Her confidence cuts through the dim light like a blade, but it doesn't ease the knot coiled in Ceige's chest. "I remember the map too, you know. Maintenance tunnels—quieter, cleaner. No alarms."

Quieter? Cleaner? Ceige drags a breath through her teeth. The thought of those cramped, suffocating corridors makes her stomach lurch. "You're joking," she says, voice taut. "Pitch-black tunnels crawling with god knows what? That's your big idea?"

"Better than walking into a spotlight," Sloane shoots back, her grin widening, daring. "And since when did you care about cobwebs?" Her tone lilts upward, teasing but firm—always pushing.

Since Moscow.

Ceige exhales hard, the tension between them throbbing just under the surface. It's always like this—sharp words and sharper edges hiding something they'll never name aloud. A bond forged in violence and desperation.

"Fine," Ceige says at last, her voice clipped. "Plan A is still the elevator. The shaft is backup." Her arms fold across her chest as she leans against the booth's cool leather backing. Her thoughts scatter and reform like broken glass underfoot. "If we can't climb... we crawl."

Sloane angles forward, resting her elbows on the stained table between them. "Done my homework," she murmurs with that infuriating smirk still carved into her face. "Like I said—Eira's got surprises: piezoelectric motion sensors in the wallpaper." She lets the word hang there, savoring its absurdity.

"The wallpaper?" Ceige repeats flatly, her jaw tightening.

"Yeah." Sloane chuckles low in her throat, an almost feline sound. "Imagine that—your walls don't have ears, they have eyes."

Ceige shakes her head slowly, a bitter laugh escaping before she can stop it. "Well... if anyone can shut it down," she mutters reluctantly, "it's you."

"Exactly!" Sloane's voice lifts with mock triumph, coaxing a faint grin out of Ceige despite herself. Shadows dance across Sloane's face as she leans closer. "Intercepted signals are easy if you know what to grab—and lucky for us..." She spreads her hands out like an offering.

Ceige narrows her eyes at her partner but doesn't interrupt.

"I swiped a 783 off some Underground vendor last week," Sloane continues casually—too casually—like confessing petty crime over coffee. "Thing was just sitting there all lonely in its case." A sly nudge against Ceige's shoulder punctuates her words.

Ceige doesn't laugh this time; instead, she shifts back to strategy mode—the only tether keeping their reckless venture intact. "Alright," she says lowly, each syllable deliberate. "The X-9 handles biometric locks first thing—that's non-negotiable." Her gaze hardens as she adds: "If Eira senses us coming... we're dead before we even get close."

"No arguments here," Sloane replies smoothly and leans further in—the glint in her eye brighter now than before as if danger itself fuels some hidden fire inside of her. "Once we're in," she whispers conspiratorially, "I disable the sensors—easy-peasy."

Ceige arches a brow but lets it slide—for now.

"And after that?" Sloane presses lightly but eagerly—a predator circling its prey yet pretending to play nice for another moment longer. "We don't walk in waving weapons around." Somewhere beneath those words lies something else unspoken: They've already crossed too many lines; there's no turning back anymore—not even if they wanted to.

Disruption.

Chaos unleashed.

"Draw their eyes away," Ceige says. "Away from us, away from the real strike. Eira won't see it coming. A NeuroPick A-1 will handle that."

Sloane's voice cuts through the scheming. "Destruction?" Her lips curl into something sharp, her eyes sharpened steel. "I like destruction. But let me ask—can I be the one to kill her?"

"Why?" Ceige asks.

"Cass." Sloane answers, steady, firm.

No hesitation.

"Yes."

The word hangs in the air between them like a blade suspended by a thread.

Sloane nods once. Silence follows, broken only by the low hum of the Underground and the faint scrape of napkin against wood as their scrawled plans sit there between them—lines and ink promising violence on paper.

"Ready?" Sloane asks finally. Light words, but there's weight beneath them, heavy as stone.

"Let's get it done," Ceige says. Her pulse quickens; she feels it echo in her chest, in her fingertips. The mission looms over them, vast and unforgiving. Stakes high enough to choke on, odds slim enough to cut skin—but for a fleeting moment, shared purpose is gravity anchoring her resolve.

"Burn it," Sloane says flatly, flicking her lighter open and holding it out.

Ceige doesn't take it. Instead, she grabs the napkin without a word and drops it into her glass of whiskey. Ink blooms outward in dark tendrils before dissolving entirely, washing their plans away in amber liquid. She thumbs the X-9 pen tucked between her fingers—a flicker of blue light—and watches as the last remnants liquefy into sludge at the bottom of her drink.

She raises the glass to the flame and mutters under her breath, "Cheers." The whiskey is fire on its way down; she swallows it without flinching. "Thanks for the light."

Sloane smirks as if she owns the room, leaning back into her seat with arms crossed in easy defiance. "Didn't know you moonlighted as a spy bartender."

Ceige cuts her off sharply before the smirk can spread further. "Don't get cocky."

Her voice is flat steel—not harsh but firm enough to make Sloane's confidence pause mid-step. Still, there's something about that swagger—brash and unshaken—that presses against Ceige's edges like heat against ice. Confidence so bright it almost feels contagious.

Almost.

But not yet.

Sloane leans back farther now, smirk returning like old habit etched into bone. "Always so serious." Her tone is light but teasing only skims the surface; something colder lingers underneath. Her head tilts as if measuring Ceige with fresh amusement and calculation both at once. "Fine—if we take the elevator shaft up, what's our exit plan?"

Ceige doesn't lift her eyes from where they're fixed on invisible lines she traces across the table with one finger—a slow, methodical motion that mirrors her thinking.

"The roof, outside down the building to lower levels," she says evenly. "If alarms go off... we move fast." A pause as if weighing each step before she continues: "Avoid main security."

Sloane grins wide now—a reckless grin like a gambler spreading cards across felt—and there's something maddeningly vibrant about it that makes Ceige's pulse twitch against her ribs again despite herself.

"Fast and messy, headlong down the outside of the building," Sloane echoes with an air of careless delight that sets Ceige's teeth on edge. She shrugs casually like none of this matters—as though lives don't hang in balance or failure isn't waiting just around some blind corner ahead of them somewhere up top in that building where Eira waits behind layers of guards and locked doors.

"I like it."

The winds howl.

Raw and unforgiving.

Cryosium's breath, Ceige thinks, sucks out marrow.

They sit hunched in a dim booth, the bar a smoky cave of murmurs and flickering neon. The Underground hums with life—snatches of hollow laughter, deals whispered over battered tables. Outside, the wind screams; inside, the air crackles.

"What about setting off the alarms on purpose?" Sloane's voice is low but sharp, cutting through Ceige's thoughts like a blade. "A distraction to keep Eira's dogs looking the other way while we slip upstairs."

Ceige nods once. Quick. Sharp. "Chaos works. But we'll have to move faster than her response teams."

Sloane waves a hand, dismissive, as if brushing away the weight of contingencies. Her grin fades just enough to reveal what lies beneath—steel. "We've got this if we stick together."

Ceige watches her for too long. Something in those words presses against a part of herself she doesn't want to touch. A weight she can't name but feels all the same. When she finally speaks, her voice is quiet but solid: "Right."

Sloane grins again, wide and wild, and their focus snaps into place like a lock clicking shut. Plans spill out between them, their voices weaving in rhythm—sharp-edged ideas sparking like flint on steel.

"What if we—" Ceige starts.

"Or we could—" Sloane interrupts.

"No, that won't work because—"

"Wait." Sloane laughs suddenly, bright and alive, her green eyes catching the dim light like shards of emerald glass. "You're overthinking again! Just trust me."

Ceige's reply comes quick and firm: "Trust isn't part of the job."

"Maybe not," Sloane says, softer now but no less certain. "But I'm going to try anyway." That smile returns—reckless, warm—and something shifts in Ceige. A crack in walls she thought would never break.

She exhales through gritted teeth. "Fine," she says at last. "We'll figure it out together. But if it all goes to hell—"

"We'll go out in style." Sloane winks, her laugh cutting through the stale haze of the bar like a blade catching fire.

For a moment, neither moves. They hold each other's gaze across the table, something unspoken thrumming between them like a live wire. Outside, the winds howl louder still, raw and relentless. Inside this den of Judex—their refuge and their trap—the noise softens to a hum. Between them burns something small but stubborn—a flicker refusing to die in Cryosium's cold embrace.

Ceige leans back in the booth and glances down at her drink—a pool of amber flecked with soggy napkin shreds she hasn't bothered to fish out. Around them, the Underground buzzes on: laughter without warmth; murmurs without promises.

Her attention stays fixed on Sloane.

"We need the NeuroPick A-1," Ceige says at last, her voice low but steady as a blade drawn slow from its sheath. "It's our only shot at cracking Eira's security."

Sloane straightens in her seat at once; her curls tumble wild across her face as her eyes gleam with something sharp and familiar—mischief clothed in certainty.

"The East Wall stall?" she asks with a tilt of her head. "They've got everything."

"Yeah." Ceige leans forward now; tension coils tight under her skin like wire about to snap. "But if we want one before anyone else does—"

"We move now."

"Race you."

Sloane's grin slices through the dim light, sharp as broken glass. Before Ceige can reach for her, she's gone—a flash of leather and reckless motion vanishing into the crowd.

"Wait—"

But the word dies on Ceige's lips. Sloane is already carving a path through bodies and smoke, her silhouette dissolving, reappearing, slipping between tables like liquid shadow. For a single breath, Ceige lingers. Then she moves.

Her boots slam the ground. Hard. Fast. Chasing after that laugh—that bright, defiant laugh that cuts through the bar's haze like a blade drawn across skin.

"Not fair!" Ceige yells, dodging a cluster of hunched figures murmuring low over a deal about to sour. Sloane doesn't glance back. She doesn't need to. Her laughter hangs in the air, bold and untouchable, daring Ceige to follow.

Neon flickers overhead—sickly greens and cold blues flashing on brick walls slick with frost and grime. The bar folds into shadow after shadow, each one darker than the last, but Ceige keeps moving. And there's Sloane ahead of her—wild-eyed, unrelenting—like none of this can touch her.

For a moment—a heartbeat—the weight of Cryosium falls away.

"Catch me if you can!" The shout tears from Sloane's mouth like lightning cracking against stone. It hits Ceige square in the chest—a challenge laced with something deeper. Rawer. Her pulse surges as she drives forward, closing the space between them inch by inch.

The Underground market opens around them without warning—a labyrinth of broken stalls and cracked alleyways bleeding cold. Shadows coil around scrap metal and rusted tech piled high on battered tables. The air cuts sharp here—sharp enough to bite—but Ceige doesn't slow.

Sloane glides ahead like she owns the chaos.

Like the cold and noise can't break her.

"Keep up!" she hollers over her shoulder, her grin flashing again—this time a taunt wrapped in firelight and daring.

Ceige doesn't answer at first. Words take too much breath she can't spare—not when each exhale blooms in frozen clouds before her face. Her boots crunch against frost-shattered stone as she skirts an overturned crate, her body weaving through debris and indifferent vendors who barely blink at their game of pursuit.

All motion now.

All instinct.

For just a second—for less than that—it feels like freedom.

Don't think about Cryosium or jagged ceilings threatening to collapse above it all. Don't think about survival squeezing you into tighter spaces every day until you vanish completely.

Just run.

And then: "Don't get cocky." The mocking words burst from her lips with a half-smirk trailing behind them as she surges forward again, faster this time, cutting dangerously close to a stall laden with twisted copper wire and shattered glass displays.

Ahead of them looms their target—a dingy table swallowed by shadows at the far edge of chaos—and its faint glow hums with promise: exactly what they came for.

Almost there.

Sloane surges ahead.

A laugh—sharp, jagged. Like glass breaking in an empty room.

"What's wrong? Too slow?"

Ceige fires back.

"Watch yourself."

Her voice steady, though her legs burn like wires sparking in a storm. She grins—teeth bared, bright, cutting—as she pulls closer. Every breath between them charged, their rivalry a razor-edge tension. Competition and camaraderie tangled together, impossible to separate.

The vendor sees them coming.

His eyes widen.

Panic replaces boredom as he scrambles to shield his wares. Two figures tearing toward him like stray bullets.

Neither Ceige nor Sloane slows down.

They push harder. Faster. Two forces hurtling toward collision.

"Winner takes all!" Ceige barks, her words slicing the air as she pulls alongside Sloane.

Sloane glances sideways—grin wild, reckless.

"Deal."

The moment snaps tight as they reach for the same prize in unison. Cold metal under their fingertips.

Neutron stars collide.

Kilonova.

Their bodies crash together—a collision that rattles bones and steals breath. Neither shatters, neither falls. They remain suspended in that violent fusion, drunk on the raw force of impact, two stars burning brighter in their collision.

"Damn," Ceige says, mostly in admiration.

Sloane steps forward first.

Fluid, confident, untouchable.

She smirks—a blade unsheathed—and points down at the NeuroPick lying on the vendor's display.

"How much?"

The vendor glares at her from beneath furrowed brows. Wary now. "Two hundred credits."

"Two hundred?" Sloane's laugh is soft yet sharp enough to cut. "For this? I've seen better up in the Upper District—for half that."

"Then go buy it there," the vendor snaps, already half-turned away.

Sloane doesn't blink.

She leans casually against the counter as if it were hers already, her voice dropping low—smooth but with an edge that hooks him before he can walk off completely.

"Sure," she purrs, "but then my colleagues won't know about you." A pause. Calculated, heavy with meaning. "We Judex love our gear… and we talk."

Ceige hangs back now, arms crossed over her chest as she watches without interfering. Her lips twist—not a smile but something close to it—the faintest thread of amusement curling there like smoke from a distant flame. Sloane negotiates like she fights: ruthless precision wrapped in charm as thin and sharp as a wire waiting to cut through flesh.

"We talk about the good and the bad."

The vendor sighs—a low hiss of defeat—as he finally gives her his attention again.

"One seventy-five," he mutters grudgingly.

Sloane doesn't rush the moment.

She plucks the NeuroPick A-1 off the counter and spins it lazily between her fingers like it already belongs to her—a quiet claim, undeniable yet unspoken.

"The calibration's off," she says lightly, twisting it again so its angles catch stray flashes of fluorescent light overhead. "By two degrees at least." She shrugs as though this seals its fate in stone—her matter-of-fact tone leaving no room for argument. "One twenty-five sounds right."

"You're dreaming," the vendor spits back without hesitation, though his voice is softer now than before—his earlier bravado shrinking under scrutiny he hadn't anticipated from her kind of customer. "One sixty."

"One forty," Sloane says, her voice smooth as an oiled blade. Dangerous charm glints at its edge—a weapon Ceige has learned to respect. "Word of a fair merchant's dealings echoes louder than credits down here."

The vendor's eyes narrow, his gaze a scalpel peeling back layers, searching for deceit in the tilt of her grin. Seconds stretch, pull taut. Then he nods, slow and grudging. "One fifty."

"Deal." A wink sharpens Sloane's smile as she taps the credits through. "Pleasure doing business with you."

The NeuroPick is theirs.

As they slip into the crowded arteries of the Underground, Ceige shakes her head, unable to suppress a small smirk. "You paid more than you wanted to, didn't you?"

Sloane shrugs, unbothered. "Always leave them feeling like they've won." Her grin cuts wide, teeth flashing like blades in low light. "Keeps them crawling back for more."

She hands the device off with a flick of her wrist—casual, effortless. But there's that spark in her eyes again, fleeting but electric. "Still," she says lightly, "you know I'd take bullets and guns over this kind of nonsense any day."

Ceige tucks the NeuroPick into her belt without looking at her directly. Still, a smirk betrays her. "Why am I not surprised?"

"Because you love me." The words are tossed off with playfulness, but something heavier lingers beneath them, sinking into the space between.

Ceige clears her throat like shoving that weight aside and gestures sharply ahead. "Focus."

Sloane's grin softens—not dulled but tempered—and then she adjusts the strap of her rifle. Her gaze shifts forward to where darkness gathers at the edge of vision—the kind of shadows that don't just hide things but swallow them whole. Eiskorp territory lies ahead.

Danger waits there.

Irrelevant.

The tension between them hums hotter than any threat that might be waiting in the dark.

"Alright," Sloane murmurs, testing the weight of their prize in her hand before holstering it with practiced ease.

When her green eyes flicker back toward Ceige, they burn with something fierce and resolute. "Let's get to work."

They move through the alleys like phantoms cutting through arteries drained dry of blood and life. The Underground fades behind them as sound dies by degrees—the cacophony swallowed whole by silence too sharp to be natural.

Cryosium greets them above—a slap of frost-soaked air gnawing straight through their gear, clawing skin down to bone.

"Stepping into a meat locker would be warmer," Sloane quips against the wind's bite, though frost blooms red on her cheeks and icicles cling to every word she exhales. She yanks her collar higher against it.

"Welcome topside." Ceige doesn't look at her; her focus sweeps across their surroundings—streets blackened by uneven shadows pooling like oil spills near every corner and crevice.

More danger than cover.

Sloane walks beside her—sharp energy radiating in sharp contrast to the cold pressing on all sides.

An impossible warmth in a frozen expanse.

It hums louder still.

A ghost of the market stall. A reminder of what they left behind.

"Eira won't wait all night," Ceige murmurs. Her voice barely carries over the memory of ash and flame, already fading into Cryosium's cold grip.

Sloane steps closer, her shoulder brushing against Ceige's. "So? We banging on the front door? Ask to use their elevator?"

The faintest smirk flickers across Ceige's face before fading, her eyes steady on the path ahead. "Not unless you want to see what the inside of a Cryosium cell looks like."

"Got it," Sloane says, dropping low in an exaggerated crouch. "Stealth mode engaged." Her boots skid slightly on the frost-slick street as she pretends to creep along, a deliberate absurdity in this landscape of ice and shadow.

"Flawless performance," Ceige replies flatly, but there's a twitch at the corner of her mouth—a spark against the relentless frost.

Sloane straightens, her breath curling in pale wisps between them. The cold wraps around their silhouettes like armor, but for just a second—for a breath—it falls away. No sound but the whisper of wind between buildings. No mission, no enemies, no Eira—just Sloane close enough to touch. Just an unspoken something neither of them dares to name.

Then Ceige turns. Abrupt. Sharp. Whatever lingered between them severed by motion alone. "Let's move."

Her boots crunch against frozen pavement as she leads them forward into Cryosium's unforgiving night. The cold cuts deep—sharpened knives slicing through fabric and skin—but she doesn't falter. Doesn't look back.

Behind them, The Underground disappears into shadow, swallowed whole by the vastness above. Ahead, the city rises like a predator coiled to strike—silent streets heavy with unseen eyes.

Sloane pushes through the wind at her side, shrugging off strands of hair that whip free in the storm's fury. She laughs softly—carelessly—and it cuts through Cryosium's frozen air like light breaking through shadow.

"Why are you laughing," Ceige says and doesn't ask. "Dying isn't funny."

"What can I say?" Sloane's eyes gleam like burial lights. "Some of us are already ghosts."

Ceige feels it then—that laugh, that spark—the way it pulls something loose inside her for half a heartbeat before she tears herself free again and keeps walking.

Snow carves lines in their faces as they breach another street: Eiskorp's domain dead ahead.

Metal.

Frost.

Move.

"Hell of a blizzard," Sloane mutters under her breath as she steadies her weapon against her shoulder. "Like she's pulling strings on the damn weather itself."

"But she doesn't control us."

Ceige tightens the straps on her gear, muscles taut, ready to spring. A coiled predator. "Ready?"

Sloane grins, a flash of heat against the frost. "Born ready."

"Three. Two. One."

They explode forward.

Boots slam against the ice-slick ground. The air bites at their lungs, sharp as broken glass. Each step is a battle through the frozen sludge clawing at their legs, but they drive onward. The pull of their mission is stronger than the cold. Stronger than fear.

"Think we'll end up as popsicles if we screw this up?" Sloane yells, her tone light, but the edges fray under strain.

"Only if we don't get out." Ceige cuts her a quick glance and catches it—Sloane's fire, burning fierce against the storm. Her breath hangs in pale clouds that twist and vanish in the swirling snow. And for a fleeting moment, Ceige's heart stammers—not just from the run or the cold, but from something electric. Something raw and reckless that defies reason.

They cut left—an alley, narrow and claustrophobic, swallowing them whole in its shadowed maw. Darkness stretches long fingers across crumbling brick walls, trying to ensnare them. But together? Together they're untouchable. Two Judex carving paths through chaos.

Ceige sees it then—a flicker of wrongness in the dark. A shadow moves where it shouldn't.

Her body reacts faster than thought.

"Sloane—stop!"

But too late.

The guard surges from the black like a phantom made flesh. Ceige throws out an arm and slams Sloane aside before she can fully register what's happening. They hit hard—the snow rises to claim them in an icy embrace.

The guard swings up his weapon—

A single crack shatters the silence.

The man drops back into the snow's grasp as if pulled by unseen hands. Sloane lowers her arm, smoke curling faintly from her gun barrel like breath on the frozen wind.

"Loser," she mutters with a smirk, brushing herself off as though she hadn't just ended a life with perfect precision.

Ceige staggers upright, heart hammering, adrenaline coiling hot beneath her skin. It's not about survival anymore—it's about holding onto something fragile that beats just beneath all this chaos.

The silence crashes back down around them like an avalanche, heavy and suffocating. The guard lies still in the drifts, his blood slowly staining white into red.

No time to linger.

Ahead looms Eira's fortress—a jagged silhouette rising against an unforgiving sky.

"Let's go," Sloane says, voice deceptively calm even as her breath mists around her lips in icy ghosts.

Ceige nods sharply, snow sliding from her sleeves as she sets off beside her partner once more—into the unrelenting freeze waiting just ahead.

Chapter 9

Artificial.

Strong.

Stronger.

The wind bites. Cold and sharp, it slashes through the alley like a scalpel, carving through layers of clothing, flesh, bone. It's unnatural. Ceige crouches low against the concrete, her breath hanging pale in the frozen air before vanishing into nothing. The ice-encrusted wall presses against her shoulder as she powers up the NeuroPick A-1. The device hums, soft and steady, before the laser ignites—a thin blade of light that melts through ice and stone as if they weren't even there.

Sloane watches from a few paces back, arms folded tightly across her chest, her coat whipping in the wind like an angry flag. Her hair lashes her face, but she doesn't seem to notice. "That thing isn't going to ricochet and fry me into ash, is it?" she asks, voice flat but loud enough to cut through the howl of the air around them. "I'd prefer not to combust before we hit go."

"Eyes on the perimeter," Ceige says without looking up. Her fingers tighten around the tool as she adjusts its angle. The laser works with surgical precision, the concrete cracking in neat slices that crumble at her feet. She feels adrenaline spike—hot and electric—coursing past the cold that has sunk into her fingers and toes. This is routine for her. For Sloane? It's something else entirely.

"Sure thing." Sloane gives a crooked smirk, teeth flashing white against the storm's gray haze. "Miss Ice-in-Her-Veins strikes again." She shifts her weight from one foot to the other, scanning their surroundings with casual disinterest that Ceige knows better than to believe is real. "Nothing gets your blood pumping like an industrial-strength party laser."

"All according to plan," Ceige growls, cutting a glance over her shoulder just as the last chunk of concrete falls away. Beneath it yawns an opening—a narrow corridor framed by walls of sterile white light that flicker faintly like dying stars. Cold air drifts upward from it in a shallow exhale that chills more than any winter wind could ever manage.

Ceige straightens slowly, eyes narrowing at what waits.

Sloane steps forward first—quick movements, deliberate and measured despite the grin tugging at her lips—and glances back over her shoulder with one of those signature winks that drives Ceige insane in ways she doesn't have time to unpack right now. "After you," she murmurs lightly, though something in her tone hints at tension coiled beneath all that bravado.

Ceige doesn't answer; she just moves past Sloane and into the corridor without hesitation, boots crunching softly against frost-coated concrete as she goes deeper into the white-lit void.

Sloane follows close behind, already pulling out her 783 device like it's part of her hand instead of just another piece of tech strapped to her body. Her fingers fly across its surface, quick and sure despite the cold stiffening the air around them. "Let's disappear," she whispers under her breath as she activates the NFC override with a faint pulse that ripples invisibly outward.

The shift is instant—an unseen bubble wrapping itself around them both like armor made of absence and shadow—and when Sloane clips the device to her collar with a satisfied click, there's no trace left behind for any watching eyes or ears to find.

"Stay inside my radius," she says softly but firmly, emerald eyes locking onto Ceige's for half a second longer than necessary before flicking away again toward something unseen in the distance ahead of them.

Ceige nods once—sharp and brisk—and starts forward again without another word. Sloane matches pace easily beside her this time, footsteps falling into rhythm against floors that stretch too long and too bright beneath buzzing lights overhead.

The sound echoes around them: hollow and endless.

"I don't know about you," Sloane murmurs after a moment—her voice pitched low now like talking too loud might wake something waiting just beyond their line of sight—"but this feels exactly like walking straight into some B-grade horror flick."

"We are walking into some B-grade horror flick," Ceige answers evenly without breaking stride or turning back toward Sloane at all because stopping now isn't an option—not when every muscle in her body is screaming danger with every step forward—but there's an edge to her voice that cuts anyway: raw anticipation buried under layers of practiced calm.

Sloane grins wide at that—sharp-edged but genuine—and there's no mistaking how much pleasure she takes from whatever chaos lies ahead when she says softly but firmly enough for both of them to hear clearly: "Bullets and bloodshed, baby."

And just like that—as if summoned by those words alone—the lights overhead flicker again before dimming entirely for one long breathless second that feels like falling into forever itself.

The air bites.

Cold, sharp, sterile.

A hollow chill wraps around them, clinging like frost to their bones as they descend farther into Eiskorp's belly.

"Save your bullets for when we find Eira," Ceige says, her voice low, slicing through the heavy quiet like a blade drawn from its sheath. Not just a warning—an anchor. Something solid to hold onto as the walls tighten and the shadows deepen.

The air stings their throats, an antiseptic miasma laced with something fouler beneath. Acrid. Metallic. Wrong. The stench of corrupted power, decaying in its own arrogance.

Sloane shivers, rubbing her arms through her gloves. "Hell's frozen over in here," she mutters, her breath curling like smoke in the icy air.

Ceige glances ahead, her expression carved from stone, but there's something faint—a smirk that flickers and dies in an instant. "Get used to it," she says. "Consider it practice for when everything goes to hell."

"Practice? I think this is hell, it's just frozen over," Sloane echoes with a brittle laugh that cracks on the edges and falls flat. The sound scatters against the ice-slick walls and disappears into nothingness, swallowed whole by the sterile void around them.

Ceige doesn't laugh. Doesn't answer either. Her eyes sweep over every shadow that crawls along the walls under harsh white light—shadows that slither like snakes biding their time. Nothing moves right here. Not the dark. Not the air. Not even time itself.

"Focus," Ceige says finally, her voice cold steel wrapped tight around tension. "This isn't a game."

No reply now from Sloane—just a sharp exhale as they push deeper into the labyrinth of frost and silence. Two shadows moving as one through corridors lined with frostbitten walls and unseen malice. Vengeance drives them forward. Desperation keeps them steady.

At last, they reach it—the terminal is there before them like an altar to some desolate machine god, humming softly with cold light. Ceige drops to one knee without hesitation, her gloved fingers darting across the glowing interface. The holographic display flares to life in a sudden burst of icy blue, casting spectral light over her face—a mask caught between exhaustion and determination.

The X-9 buzzes faintly in her grasp, its pulse steady as a heartbeat—if machines could bleed life into this frozen necropolis.

Behind her, Sloane hovers like something untamed—a restless ghost pacing at the edge of unraveling nerves. Her boots scrape softly against metal flooring, each step sharp and grating in the silence. "How long can you keep that up?" she hisses at last.

"As long as I need to," Ceige answers without looking back, her tone flat as the frozen ground beneath them. Her focus stays locked ahead as code peels away layer by layer—an intricate dissection of digital flesh stripped down to bare bone.

Sloane doesn't press further.

The shadows don't stop slithering.

The cold doesn't bite any less deeply.

And vengeance waits ahead like a beast finally stirred awake.

"We don't have all night."

Sloane's voice cuts through the stillness, sharp-edged, carrying adrenaline splintered with unease.

"Stop pacing," Ceige snaps, a whisper wrapped in steel. Shadows flicker across her face as she stares down the digital wall in front of her, the shifting glow from the console carving out hollows under her eyes—marks left by sleepless nights and wars fought in places no one remembers anymore.

Sloane halts mid-step but can't be still. Her fingers twitch against the strap on her belt, restless, her other hand gripping her weapon so tightly it seems fused to her skin. The silence wraps around them—not calm, not empty, but coiled, alive, waiting to strike like something feral biding its time.

"This place..." Sloane murmurs into the thickness of it all. "It's too quiet." Her words barely carry past her lips, but they don't need to—what she feels is already crawling up their spines like ice burying itself beneath flesh.

"Maybe they're taking five," Ceige mutters as another firewall crumbles beneath her hands. The sarcasm hangs brittle in the air, thin armor over the tension etched into every line of her body.

"Or watching us right now," Sloane counters. Her smirk is faint and fractured—a mask that cracks under pressure but doesn't shatter. Anxiety gnaws at the edges of her voice; bravado only stretches so far before it snaps.

The last barrier breaks—shattered code falling away like dust from a forgotten boneyard. The console pulses green: access granted.

Ceige straightens sharply, holstering the X-9. "We're in." Two words, flat and uncelebratory, more fact than triumph.

They move as one now—phantoms threading their way through corridors that twist into something unreal with every step forward. Frost slicks the ground beneath them; each footfall whispers muted defiance against the cold sheen below. Overhead, fluorescent lights drone like distant wasps trapped inside glass jars—an incessant buzz that needles into exposed nerves.

Shadows slither along walls burnt sickly yellow by years of relentless light; they stretch too long, bend at strange angles. Everything here feels off—sterile yet suffocating, vast yet claustrophobic—like reality itself is warped and watching them back from somewhere just beyond sight.

The corridor yawns open ahead of them—a hollow void of polished frost and mechanical hums echoing like faint screams buried under steel and circuitry. Its doors are sentinels lining either side: faceless slabs of metal and frosted glass keeping secrets locked tight.

"How's it this empty?" Sloane breathes at last, eyes darting between shifting shadows as though expecting one to leap forward and take shape. "This place is a goddamn fortress."

"Corporate greed doesn't need an audience," Ceige replies coolly without looking at her; her gaze sweeps instead over angles and exits—tracing escape routes for threats she knows might already be moving beneath the silence.

Sloane snorts softly, bitterly. "Guess they don't want anyone seeing what kind of nightmare they're bankrolling."

"Focus." Ceige doesn't snap this time—it's quieter than that but cuts sharper all the same: quick as a blade drawn clean and fast through air. For half a second there's something resembling amusement tugging faintly at her mouth before it vanishes again behind iron resolve.

"We're not here to play judge," she says softly—and then keeps walking forward into shadows that seem to pull tighter around them with every step.

The light is wrong.

Too bright. Too cold.

It spills across the polished floors in sterile sheets, chasing them as they move deeper into the unknown. Their footsteps make no sound.

A corner looms ahead.

And then it hits them.

Sloane freezes. Her hand shoots out, clutching Ceige's arm in a bruising grip. "What is that?" she whispers, the words trembling loose from her throat.

Ceige doesn't answer. Can't. Her eyes track Sloane's stunned gaze to the chamber ahead, and her breath falters.

The laboratory yawns open before them—a vast, cavernous thing under clinical fluorescence. Silence hangs heavy, smothering, as though the room itself has forgotten how to breathe. Glass tanks rise like monoliths from the floor, towering over them, their smooth surfaces gleaming with a predator's indifference. Shadows twist and warp on the walls behind them, grotesque parodies of the figures within.

Inside the tanks—things.

No longer human.

Twisted shapes drift suspended in viscous amber fluid. Limbs contorted. Faces locked mid-scream, frozen in anguish that seems to echo through the oppressive quiet. Their hollowed eyes stare back, accusing and empty, and Ceige feels the air leave her lungs all at once.

Sloane inhales sharply beside her, a ragged breath that shudders against the weight of what she's seeing. Her body stiffens; fists ball at her sides. For a long moment, she says nothing.

Then: "What the hell is this?"

Her voice is a thread pulled taut—a tremor riding its surface—but it cuts through the silence like breaking glass.

"Boundaries," Ceige murmurs eventually. The word tastes bitter on her tongue. She forces herself to take another step forward—closer to those monstrous silhouettes trapped behind glass—and feels her composure slip with every inch she closes. Humanity reduced to this. Broken and mangled beyond recognition for profit masquerading as progress. "Or what's left when they're crossed."

Sloane moves toward one of the tanks as if drawn by gravity itself. She stops inches away, her hand hovering just shy of touching the glass. Her fingers tremble ever so slightly.

She stares into sunken eyes clouded with despair. Sees herself reflected there.

"They didn't ask for this," she whispers finally, raw and tight, each word carved from stone.

"Neither did we."

Ceige's voice is soft but distant—cool as frost spreading thin over a windowpane—and yet something stirs beneath it. A flicker of recognition she doesn't want to let in but can't quite shut out.

Sloane spins toward her then, anger blazing sudden and fierce in those wide brown eyes, a stark flame against the cold sterility of their surroundings. "Look at them!" Her voice slashes through the air like a knife drawn in desperation. "They're not experiments—they're people! We can't just stand here."

"We have to talk about what comes next." Ceige's tone holds steady—ice meeting fire—but there's no hiding how tightly she coils herself beneath those measured words.

"Talk?" Sloane's breath catches; frustration spills over now, blistering in its intensity. "What's there to decide?" She gestures wildly toward the nearest tank—the hollowed eyes staring back from within—and her voice breaks as fury ignites into something sharper still: grief laced through with rage. "They're *people*, Ceige! Not things for some corporation to play god with!"

Ceige flinches—not outwardly but somewhere deep inside where guilt sleeps uneasy—and forces herself to meet Sloane's fire head-on. "Do you want us dead before we can do anything?"

Her words are sharp enough to sting but solid enough to anchor them both—to drag them back from whatever edge they're teetering on now.

For a moment, neither moves.

The silence presses down again.

Sloane's mask fractures.

A crack, a flicker.

Then resolve hardens over her face like cooling steel.

She pushes past Ceige, says nothing. Heavy footsteps thud into the sterile silence—each one taut with rage, each one trembling on the fragile edge of something deeper, something more breakable.

"Stay alert." Ceige's voice follows her like a shadow—flat, sharp, but lined with something softer. Concern wrapped tight in command. Her eyes cut to the tanks standing like silent sentinels along the walls. Guardians of grotesque truths.

The air shifts.

Subtle, almost nothing. But not nothing. A whisper of danger slides along Ceige's skin, tightens her nerves until they hum. The sterile atmosphere grows thick, threads pulling taut—binding them to this moment, trapping them in its tension.

"Ceige—" Sloane starts.

A crack like a rifle shot ricochets through the room.

"Sloane—don't!" Ceige calls out, her voice cutting through the sterile air, shattering it.

But Sloane doesn't stop.

The shot pierces the room—a crack of violence splitting the frozen quiet into jagged shards. Glass explodes outward; viscous fluid gushes free; twisted forms collapse into themselves as gravity drags them down like broken puppets on severed strings.

One shot becomes two.

Two becomes three.

Then all count is lost as destruction takes on rhythm and life—each pull of the trigger deliberate yet wild, each shot a scream left unspoken until now. The tanks burst one by one: liquid pooling thick and oil-slick across sterile tiles; shattered figures crumpling into heaps; steam rising briefly before surrendering to the icy chill that devours everything here.

"Goddammit, Sloane!" Ceige's voice slices through the chaos, honed sharp by fear and frustration alike. "We need to move!"

But Sloane doesn't move.

Doesn't hear her—or chooses not to.

Her eyes linger on the wreckage: thick fluids running cold, once-warm vapor vanishing into Cryosium's ruthless frost. Life extinguished without ceremony, warmth swallowed whole by unyielding ice. Fitting, she thinks—or maybe she doesn't think at all—just watches it fade into frozen oblivion.

Sirens scream.

Red pulses, red flashes.

Hell's strobe light, Ceige thinks, painting steel walls in blood.

The alarm jolts the world awake, a harsh symphony of sound and light. The floor shakes—boots pounding, thunder rolling, an army rushing forward with the inevitability of a storm. Ceige doesn't turn to look. There's no time for regret now, no room for reflection. Only survival. Only the moment.

Ruins surround them—red from the sirens, white from winter's breath creeping through cracks in shattered glass. Snow and steel. Blood and frost.

"Shit, shit, shit," Sloane snarls under her breath. Her boots skid on icy grating, the sound of desperation scraping against metal. Ceige tightens her grip on her gun; it's sleek in her hand, a black weight humming with restrained violence.

"Positions," Ceige says. Her voice is taut wire, snapping tension into action.

They move like magnets drawn to charged poles—fluid but deliberate. Defensive stances as natural as breathing. Muscles tense. Condensed breaths hang in the air like ghosts of words unsaid. Time presses in around them, heavy and cold. Violence presses harder.

"How many?" Sloane's question cuts through the void between them; her eyes are alight with reckless hunger, a spark yearning to catch fire.

Ceige doesn't hesitate. "Too many."

Die!

Sloane screams it, throat raw, the word tearing loose like a blade. The bodies collapse—broken, crumpled. Dark streaks smear the lab's white, sterile void. Blood blooms on the floor like flowers blooming fire.

"I'm using the laser," Ceige says, the words flat but sharp-edged with something unspoken. The A-1 hums to life. A searing beam cuts through flesh without hesitation.

Sloane laughs. Harsh, splintered laughter, jagged as glass smashing against steel. She slams another clip into place. "Your laser's a masterpiece."

Ceige doesn't answer. She steps forward, boots crunching on remains slick with ruin, toward the elevator at the end of the hall—a monolith of cold metal cutting into darker silence. Behind them, carnage pools across tile and steel. Shadows cast by shattered lives stretch long in their wake.

History carves itself here—not in books, not in ink—but in blood and frostbitten memory.

No one will forget.

Chapter 10

Eira's penthouse breathes death.

Silent. Cold. Coiled.

The storm outside is a living thing, its frozen breath seething, trying to get in. The building rises into it like a shard of ice, jagged and unyielding. Snow drifts through unseen fractures, gathering in corners like forgotten regrets. Frost creeps across steel and leather, etching patterns as intricate—and as cruel—as their architect. This place isn't a home. It's a statement.

Eira's brutality made concrete.

Ceige freezes mid-step, her breath sharp in her throat. The marble floor gleams too cleanly—too flawlessly smooth. A trick of the light catches her eye: faint, predatory glimmers crouched within the surface. Pressure sensors. Ceige throws an arm out, slamming it into Sloane's chest and yanking her back before their weight tips the trap.

"Hold," she whispers, the word fraying into the air like frost blown from steel.

Sloane doesn't flinch; she never does. Just grins—sharp, careless, maddening as always. "Nice catch," she murmurs, that damn smirk curling across her face again.

The quiet doesn't last.

A sound rises—a low whine that cuts through stillness like a blade drawn across stone. Panels split open with unnatural grace, revealing turrets nestled deep like golden serpents coiled to kill. Their lasers flare to life—thin red beams slicing shadows apart like veins spilling light into darkness.

"Down," Ceige snaps, her voice flat and unshaking even as chaos ignites around them.

Gunfire erupts—a brutal cadence that fills the room with thunder and heat. Light strobes off jagged edges of glass and steel as Ceige dives low, rolling through the hailstorm of bullets. Her A-1 hums awake in her hands, its edge glowing faintly—a blade restrained but eager.

Sloane moves like wildfire—too fast for recklessness to catch up with her yet. She vaults over a chaise without hesitation, momentum carrying her fluidly forward, wild laughter cracking through gunfire like lightning splitting open the sky. "Always wondered what it'd feel like to star in my own deathtrap!" she shouts over the roar of metal and fury.

Ceige grits her teeth but doesn't answer—not while fire rips at their heels and sparks claw at their skin. Leave it to Sloane to flirt with death while laughing in its face.

The turrets move too—precision incarnate. Their targeting systems hum with hunger, punishing every misstep with bursts of searing red fire that gouge molten scars into the floor where flesh should have stood. Ceige's mind races ahead of her body—calculating distances, predicting trajectories—but instinct drives where reason hesitates.

Then she sees it—a gap between twin arcs of crimson death no wider than breath itself.

"Now!" she shouts, her voice splintering against noise and fear as she shoves Sloane toward the opening without waiting for an argument.

Ceige twists away just as fire obliterates where they both had been standing a blink ago. Her shoulder hits polished marble hard—she feels it scrape through uniform and skin—but there's no time for pain or anger or regret. Her A-1 growls in her grip again like an animal stirring beneath its leash but she doesn't aim yet—not with Sloane moving so wildly through lines of fire that any shot could turn fatal by inches.

And then comes a new sound—the heavy puncture of boots breaking ice-crusted glass.

They land together: two figures armored head-to-toe in chrome exosuits that catch fragments of stormlight spilling through shattered windows behind them. The storm howls louder now—its voice trapped within this frozen monastery as those two men rise to their full height like statues come alive only to kill.

Deliberate steps echo across frost-rimed marble floors—they're steady but coiled tight as wire straining before the snap.

Ceige doesn't blink.

Inhumanity lives here after all—and tonight it wears chrome skin.

"Finally," Sloane says, her voice light, almost playful. The kind of playful that comes with sharp edges. She raises her pistol, eyes narrowing—a glint in that vivid green, caught between mischief and something darker. "Shall we dance?"

Ceige doesn't answer. She moves.

Low.

The kick whistles just above her head—a near miss—but she's already rising, A-1 blade cutting upward in a clean, deliberate arc. Synthetic flesh parts like fabric under strain. Sparks spit from the wound. A groan of machinery failing itself. The guard crumples. Heavy. Lifeless. Like wet snow collapsing on itself before it hits the ground.

Gunfire cracks behind her—two shots, sharp and precise.

Sloane's work.

The second guard staggers back, armor buckling at its weakest seams. Another shot folds him; his body hits and stays down. The silence that follows is sudden, thick as smoke in a closed room.

"Routine maintenance," Sloane says, breath lighter now but tinged with satisfaction. Her gaze sweeps the carnage: bodies sprawled like discarded mannequins, blood pooling slow and dark against the polished floor.

"Don't tempt fate," Ceige cuts in, voice level but taut as wire drawn tight enough to snap. Her eyes stay forward, scanning—noticing the wrongness of the quiet. It presses in, oppressive as storm clouds heavy with thunder waiting to break.

"Where's the fun in playing it safe?" Sloane grins as she reloads her pistol in one smooth motion.

Ceige doesn't smile back. Almost does.

Outside, wind claws at the skyscraper's windows, rattling its steel bones. Snow swirls in wild spirals—chaotic patterns matching what lies inside.

"Eyes up," Ceige mutters low but firm, knuckles tightening on the weapon that anchors her to this moment. The cold weight of it steadies her thoughts as tension builds—subtle but growing, like heat rising beneath a frozen surface ready to crack wide open.

Then it happens.

A blur of movement—erratic and wrong—bursts into view like a puppet flung by its strings. The third guard emerges, his steps jerky and desperate: part man, part machine straining past its limits. Wires coil beneath pale skin stretched too tight; his augmented muscles twitch unnaturally even as he surges forward with alarming speed.

Toward Sloane.

"Behind you!"

Ceige's shout is sharp—a single note cutting through thick air. No hesitation now: the A-1 hums faintly in her grip as its laser edge arcs again—brief brilliance cutting through chaos.

The strike lands cleanly.

A hiss escapes from severed tendons and ruptured circuits—a sound sharp and final as frost cracking beneath weight too heavy for it to hold. The augmented guard stumbles mid-lunge before falling hard, spasms rattling his frame as errant sparks dance across ruined joints.

He twitches once more before stillness takes him entirely—a lifeless heap amid the quiet storm gathering both outside and within.

Sloane grins. Wide. Unbothered.

"That's one way to handle it."

No time for celebration. Victory, ephemeral as smoke in the wind. Another shadow shifts, a flicker in the chaos of shattered consoles and dying lights.

"Keep moving," Ceige snaps, her voice sharp, unyielding. She pivots behind Sloane, steps falling into the rhythm they know so well. Muscle memory takes over—survival etched into their bones, bloodshed carved into their souls. Every movement feels inevitable, every action honed to a deadly edge.

"Two o'clock! Left flank!" Ceige doesn't shout; she doesn't need to. Her voice cuts through the din, clear as steel slicing air.

Sloane answers with a grin, infuriatingly confident even now. "Got it."

They move as one—a brutal symphony of gunfire and relentless motion slicing through the penthouse shadows. Here, in this shattered cathedral of tech and death, they are unstoppable. A grotesque ballet unfolds across tiles slick with oil and blood, bodies broken and scattered like discarded refuse from some macabre machine. Bullets streak through the air like falling stars, burning bright before they die against walls of cold steel and clawing shadows.

Outside, the storm howls like a wounded beast, its fury battering the glass that separates them from the chaos beyond.

Sloane drops another hostile without hesitation—her weapon barks once, twice, defiant against the rising tide of threats. "This is it? Eira's sending scraps at us now? Starting to feel insulted."

"Less talking," Ceige growls through clenched teeth, her eyes raking over every corner shrouded in smoke and ruin. The bodies at their feet are victory and warning all at once—a tightening noose with every kill, each heartbeat drawing them closer to an end they can't yet see but can feel creeping toward them.

The air shifts—something massive stirs just outside their reach. Heavy tension vibrates through the room like an unspoken promise of violence yet to come.

Sloane fires again.

Pft.

The last guard crumples against a mahogany desk, his augmented limbs spasming as sparks dance around his corpse before fading to silence. Ceige's gaze locks with Sloane's—no words pass between them, just a shared understanding steeped in dread and determination. Two parts fear; one part fury.

"Barely broke a sweat," Sloane murmurs, but there's no levity in her voice now—her brow furrows under the weight of something darker.

"Don't kid yourself," Ceige replies, low and sharp like a blade buried under velvet cloth. The quiet hums with unease, thick enough to choke on. Nothing about this feels right—not here, not now.

And then it comes.

The voice cuts through the stillness like a razor laid against skin:

"Did you really think you could corner me here?"

Cold floods the room—deeper than any winter wind screaming past the glass walls around them. Ceige tightens her grip on the A-1 at her side. It isn't just bravado she hears in that voice—it's something else entirely. A lure dragging them forward into darkness deeper than they've ever faced before.

Her heart pounds slow and heavy—a drumbeat marking time before execution.

"Set?" Sloane whispers, green eyes alight with adrenaline—and somewhere beneath it all—desperation held at bay by sheer will.

"All according to plan," Ceige answers, steady as frost coating stone; her words neither reassurance nor boast—just fact hardened by years of standing back-to-back against hell itself.

They brace together for what waits beyond the silence...

The voice comes again: sharper now—measured strokes carving through ruinous air like a scalpel through flesh:

"Sloane Vale... What a quaint surprise." A pause lingers just long enough to suffocate before it continues—a whisper twisted into mockery: "Did you truly believe you'd best me here?"

Its echoes coil off marble walls—impossible to trace... but inescapable all the same.

"You're slow," Eira says, her voice soft, slicing. "Not like Cass. She was quick—until the end." A pause, a smile sharp enough to draw blood. "Your sister fought to her last breath."

Sloane's snarl comes with the next trigger pull, each shot cracking into empty space. The bullets find only silence.

Time stretches thin, trembling like a wire ready to snap. At the far end of the room, shadows twist and ripple as if alive, peeling back to reveal her—Eira Halstead. She emerges from the dark like something summoned, like she belongs to it. Snow swirls around her, caught in the firelight. It frames her edges in flickering white and gold that can't seem to hold her still.

"Shit," Ceige mutters under her breath. Her eyes narrow as she watches Eira move—smooth, too smooth. Wrong. It's there in the way her body shifts, in a rhythm only seasoned fighters can catch. Predator's grace. Precision honed so sharp it could cut through steel.

"You want to hear Cass's last words?" Eira asks as she moves closer, as calm as if she's pacing through a garden instead of toward a fight. A cruel light glints in her eye as though plucking the memory is a game she enjoys.

Ceige doesn't wait for Sloane to answer. Her shot cracks out fast and sure—but stone chips fly where flesh should fall. Eira is gone before the bullet even knows it missed.

From across the room, Eira tilts her head at them like a teacher watching students fail a simple lesson. The corners of her mouth curl into something that isn't quite a smile but feels worse somehow—mocking, sharp-edged.

"Ceige Rivers." Her voice draws out each syllable with deliberate weight. "Stop wasting my time—or I'll make it hurt."

Sloane fires again—two rounds this time -but they pass through nothing but air.

"Sloane," Eira says lightly as she weaves between bullets that might as well have stood still for her, "she begged for you." The words come slow now, measured. Daggers meant not for flesh but for guilt itself—twisting deep before they've even landed fully.

"She didn't beg for herself," Eira goes on, softer now but no less cutting. "She begged for *you.* Sweet girl... but weak."

Sloane fires again anyway, teeth clenched so hard they might break. The shot splits the air—a crack that vanishes into useless cold and space filled only by fury and echoes.

"I can't hit her," Sloane mutters finally, low and raw like gravel grinding underfoot. She moves closer to Ceige now but keeps taut, coiled—a bowstring about to snap or shatter entirely under too much strain. Her eyes burn green-hot with anger that feels more like despair.

Ceige doesn't look at her right away. Just exhales sharp and steady like steel cooling after heat. Wordlessly raising the A-1 tucked tight against her palm, she mutters without breaking focus: "Then let's see if speed outruns light."

Her finger tightens on the trigger.

But Eira is already moving.

The room seems to shift with her—the air itself bending around what shouldn't be possible, what shouldn't exist here or anywhere else but does anyway in defiance of reason or rules or anything else they might cling to for balance.

Light catches on her eyes—not eyes at all but mirrors wrapped in frost and calculation. Every angle sharp enough to cut through hope itself.

Ceige feels the moment coming before it arrives—the wrongness of it within the air itself thickening until there's no doubt left: physics bending against them because *she* wills it so.

The laser fires searing upward—a blistering beam blazing clean through frost-laden ceiling beams while Eira remains untouched below.

Smiling still.

"Fuck," Ceige murmurs, the word slipping out like a sigh. Not anger—acceptance. They're fighting more than speed, more than enhanced reflexes. They're fighting inevitability. Synthetic flesh, neural steel. A ghost they can't touch. A phantom that fades before the bullet lands.

Eira's voice comes from somewhere in the heavy silence. Smooth, sharp. Velvet hiding a blade. "Neural enhancers are fascinating things," she says, amusement curling at the edges of her words like smoke. "Perfect recall is their gift—a theater of memory, always playing." A smile flickers across her face, thin and cold as winter light. "I think about that night often... the way she screamed your name."

Ceige fires three times before Eira finishes speaking.

She doesn't flinch.

Doesn't fall.

The bullets carve the air, but Eira isn't there when they reach her. She slides between them with a grace that hurts to watch, as though the world yields to her will and re-shapes itself around her.

Sloane hears nothing but the pounding of blood in her ears—louder even than Eira's voice as it twists and digs into her like a blade finding bone. "I made it last," Eira says, delicate, deliberate. Words like broken glass scattered with care. "Kept her aware far longer than anyone should endure." There's no cruelty in her tone—only precision, only fact. "She watched everything...right until those pretty eyes dulled."

Sloane fires again.

The shot goes wild.

Misses by miles.

Marble veins splinter across the frozen floor, fractures spidering outward like scars on skin too long left in the cold.

"Get out of your head!" Ceige barks through the haze of chaos, voice sharp enough to cut through Sloane's fury. "Don't let her win!"

But Sloane doesn't stop.

She surges forward instead, energy burning too hot to hold onto for long. Reckless abandon drives her—wild and untamed where Ceige is purpose carved down to its cleanest edge.

"I'll draw her focus!" she shouts over her shoulder without waiting for Ceige to argue or agree. Her movements are pure instinct—a storm crashing against something calm and unshakable.

"You're going to get yourself killed!" Ceige snaps after her, urgency breaking through the ice of command. Nothing reaches Sloane now—she's already gone, already rushing headlong into bright chaos and infinite cold.

Ceige breathes once—just once—and recalibrates.

Watches how Eira moves; how every step cuts through space with unerring grace; how she dances at the edge of physics where humanity can't follow. Faster than human life should be able to move. Harder than any natural thing should be able to strike.

Not just faster.

Inevitable.

Eira speaks again, and it cuts sharper than any weapon in hand or holster: "Your sister died believing in you." The words land gentle at first—but only for an instant before they bury themselves deep, jagged truths wrapped in feigned sympathy.

Each syllable precise, purposeful—a scalpel rather than a hammer.

Eira pauses, lets silence settle like frost tightening its grip on bare skin. Then comes the rest—the part meant to hollow out what's left inside: "I let her hope," she says softly, almost tenderly—almost kindly—and then wrecks it all:

"...right until she realized you weren't coming for her." Another pause—a brief moment stretched too far—before Eira leans closer with one final blow cloaked in false mercy: "She tried to cry—but those eyes were mine by then."

Sloane screams.

A fissured sound, primal and jagged. It shatters against the roar of gunfire that follows, a storm of bullets tearing through stone and shadow. Her clip burns hot in seconds, anger made audible, each shot a howl of grief carved into the world. But none of it touches flesh.

Eira flows.

Not like a fighter—like something else. Water sliding over rock. Smoke curling upward before it vanishes. Ceige watches her move, her own breath dragging sharp and cold through her lungs. The device trembles in her grip, crosshairs wavering as frustration coils tight in her chest.

She can't pin her down.

"Cover!" Ceige shouts, the word cutting past the chaos, slicing through clouds of cordite. Her hands flick over the A-1's interface, the machine humming under her touch. "Sloane, flank her!"

A reckless flash—a blur of motion. Sloane answers that call with fury blazing in her eyes, throwing herself into Eira's orbit like a comet destined to burn out. Rage propels her forward, but Ceige feels it like loss. Like blood already spilled. Each step Sloane takes is an offering on an altar built for mourning.

The A-1 thrums in Ceige's hands as she mutters to it like she can will it into perfection. "Just once," she pleads under her breath. The targeting grid locks on Eira's silhouette—a streak of impossible grace—and Ceige fires.

The beam tears through air with surgical efficiency.

Then bends.

Twists out of reality's grasp before it lands.

Eira doesn't flinch; doesn't stumble. Her gaze flashes—cold and gleaming, eyes that reflect and distort life itself. Physics bends around her as though mocked by its own limitations. The truth claws at Ceige's stomach: It won't be enough. None of this will ever be enough.

"We're outmatched," Ceige begins to say—but Eira is there already.

"You should've known better," Eira says, voice soft as silk but sharp as broken glass—the words winding their way under Ceige's armor and into her blood. Fear blooms fast and violent in its wake.

"Run!" The order bursts from Ceige as she throws herself toward cover, desperation giving it weight beyond sound or breath. The air cuts at her face now, icy against the blistering heat radiating from Eira's presence—a collision of fire and frost that fills the room with choking mist.

Steam rises around them.

Eira watches without hurry, without effort. There's a smile in her words when they come: "Let's see what you're made of."

And then she moves again—a blur so fast it ceases to be movement at all. A rhythm instead; relentless and unforgiving. Not strikes but destruction itself given form—beating its way into being one crushing blow at a time.

And they are caught inside its song.

Ceige fires.

A desperate shot. True and clean, aimed for Eira's head.

It misses.

No, not a miss. A deflection. Those blazing eyes shatter the beam's path, send it careening wild. The laser fractures upward into the ceiling, splintering plaster and wood, ricocheting like a trapped wasp. Dust spills down—thick, choking sheets that cling to every breath. Overhead, beams groan, low and mournful under sudden weight.

"Fucking hell!" Sloane curses, twisting nimbly away from falling debris—the chaos bending around her with instinctive grace.

Ceige grits her teeth. She can taste the dust. Feel panic clawing at the edges of her resolve.

"What kind of nightmare is this?" Sloane yells above the din.

"The kind no one walks away from," Ceige snaps, voice taut with urgency, "unless I make this count."

Adrenaline sharpens every nerve. Her hands tremble as she raises the weapon again—not with precision now, but desperation. Pure and unpolished. She adjusts her aim, breath stuttering against fear sharp enough to cut steel.

Another shot.

The laser screams upward again—wild, imperfect—but this time it finds something else. Not Eira. The rafters above her head.

Perfect.

The final support beam splits clean through. For a single heartbeat, the ceiling holds fast—a defiance of gravity's inevitability. Then it comes undone all at once. Concrete screams against twisted metal; rebar wrenches free with a sound like dying gods; bolts shear and give way to tons of collapsing ruin.

The world falls in waves: first the wooden beams snap like brittle twigs; then slabs of concrete break apart in violent cascades—continental plates smashing downward in chaotic reprisal. The fortress folds in on itself—splinters into a tomb of its own making.

Dust blooms upward in plumes, thick and suffocating—spinning snow into poison. Silence swells across the wreckage, heavy and absolute. But silence lies here as much as anything else does.

Something shifts beneath the rubble.

Wet movement. Then stillness.

"Stay back." Ceige's voice is sharp as breaking glass when Sloane makes to move forward—the warning cutting through the haze before she can cross what should be an end carved in stone and steel.

What should be certainty buried beneath ruinous weight.

But certainty doesn't live here. Fingers streaked in blood and dust claw their way free—a hand reaching out from beneath the rubble like something wrenched from a graveyard dream.

Ceige freezes.

"Shit." The word leaves her lips soft and thin—a cold wisp lost in freezing air as adrenaline drills through her veins like hot iron spikes driving purpose into flesh and bone. Across twisted metal and jagged stone, Eira rises—carved from shadows and firelight made flesh around smoke wreathed in steam. Her figure unwinds slow from chaos; her breath escapes her lips like dragon fire bled into winter's chill.

Her gaze locks onto Ceige—a furnace roaring too bright for mortal eyes to hold steady against it—and beneath that fire churns hunger: raw, endless hunger that gnaws at reason itself until only fury remains.

"Climb." Ceige's voice cuts through the frozen quiet as she scrambles over wreckage slick with frost and ash alike. Behind her, Sloane follows—movements shaky now beneath invisible pressure bearing down on them both like gravity turned crueler still.

They climb through ruin—a graveyard littered with fractured opulence: golden frames crushed flat underfoot; splinters of wealth ground into dust-streaked oblivion—all forgotten remembrances left behind for survival's sake alone.

"We need to go," Sloane gasps, her words cutting through the storm like jagged glass. Each breath escapes as mist in the frozen air. She glances back. "Now. Before she... resets, or whatever it is she's doing." Her gaze snaps to Eira—a firestorm behind those eyes, barely contained. A warning brewing hotter with every second.

"Up and out," Ceige growls through clenched teeth. She vaults onto a ledge glazed with ice, boots skidding just enough to make her stomach clench. A hand thrusts down, unthinking, hauling Sloane up beside her.

The storm howls.

White chaos devours the world around them. Frost claws at the air, the city below swallowed by a veil of snow and fury. Lightning splits the sky—searing flashes that turn their battlefield ghostly in electric bursts. Ceige doesn't see her so much as feel her—Eira, somewhere out there in the storm's gut. Waiting. Coiled like a viper in the shadows of snow.

"Stay sharp!" Ceige barks over the manic scream of the wind, knuckles whitening around the X-9's hilt. The A-1 is replaced by its older, smarter cousin. The holographic interface hums to life—a dim glow bleeding across her face, fragile against the tempest's ferocity.

"Always am!" Sloane shouts back, though her voice wavers under its defiance. She rolls sideways into position; every movement deliberate, precise—a dancer amid chaos. Her rifle barks twice in quick succession, shots aimed not to kill but to distract, to buy seconds they don't have. "Eira! You leave your sanity back in that fancy frost-palace?"

The storm answers with a snarl—feral, guttural, utterly wrong. Then movement—a blur gaining mass and speed until it's too fast to follow. Eira explodes forward like an avalanche unleashed—raw power forged into sleek precision. Every enhancement sharpens her into something beyond human: faster than thought, deadlier than instinct, unstoppable.

Almost.

"Watch for the lag!" Ceige shouts over the storm's roar, eyes narrowing as she tracks Eira's trajectory with surgical focus. Even machines have cracks—seams where perfection slips for just a breath too long.

There it is.

A fractional stutter in her movements—a tiny fracture between bursts of impossible velocity.

"Gotcha," Sloane mutters under her breath before diving left, laughter spilling from her lips like shattered glass scattered on stone. Her curls whip wild in the wind as she pivots mid-step and fires again—a shot that cracks through the thunderous storm like a whip snapping bone. It grazes Eira's shoulder but does little else.

Sloane grins anyway.

"If you can't stand the heat..." she shouts through clenched teeth, laughter still riding shotgun on every word, "...move to Cryosium!"

Ceige doesn't answer; she's already gone somewhere else—somewhere deep inside herself as her fingers race over the X-9's glowing surface. Lines of code hiss across its interface like static ghosts on a dying screen. Algorithms twist and writhe beneath her touch while faint light flickers like embers trying desperately not to die out.

She just needs more time—find an edge buried within those endless lines of data.

Crack this system.

Find the key.

Break Eira apart before Eira breaks them both.

It could change everything.

Or nothing at all.

"Can you even handle losing?" Sloane's voice cuts through the storm, sharp as a blade. She ducks low, bullets snapping overhead, close enough to taste the heat. Fireflies in the wind, Ceige thinks. The shots vanish into the howl of the storm, but Sloane's words do not. They hang there in the frozen air, jagged and baited with venom. "What happened to being untouchable, huh?"

Words meant to burn. Reckless words. But effective.

Eira flinches—not much, just a flicker—but it's enough for her aim to falter, her focus narrowing like a pinhole camera locking onto one thing: Sloane.

Ceige doesn't look up. She can't risk it. Her fingers hover above the flickering X-9 interface, light from the screen painting her face in shifting greens and blues. Tense jaw. Breath shallow. Teeth clenched hard enough to shatter. She studies Eira with predator's eyes, mapping every movement, every stutter in her rhythm.

There—Artillery recoils slightly in Eira's arm after every shot, a half-second lag too small for most eyes to catch but glaring in Ceige's view. Eira's augments are failing—overheating under pressure.

"She's about to find out how touchable she really is," Ceige mutters between gritted teeth. The words are barely audible under the storm screaming around them, tearing through frostbitten ruins like a feral thing unleashed. Her heart pounds against her ribs with frantic urgency—as if trying to escape its cage.

Sloane laughs—a harsh bark that echoes across frozen stone and ice-bitten steel. "Busy? Like a cat with a mouse?" Her gun cracks loud as thunder punching through cold canyon walls, striking snow on purpose instead of flesh. Not missing—choosing not to hit. Ice explodes on impact, shards flying like shattered glass caught in ribbons of fractured light.

Eira flinches again, just slightly.

But still she moves forward, mechanical precision carried on steel legs and augmented nerves: deliberate steps, gun steady and sightlines locked.

"You want to talk about Cass?" Sloane snarls now, her voice dropping lower—venom laced with something colder than the wind tearing at their coats. The teasing edge is gone; only jagged steel remains beneath that eerie calm.

Her steps change too—graceful patterns dissolving into something wild and unscripted. Less Judex now, more feral animal born of alleyways and fury. A hurricane wrapped in skin and nerve endings turned weapon against itself. No rhythm to follow; no pattern to predict.

She strikes without rhythm or reason—chaos carved into motion—and Ceige watches as Eira stumbles inside herself for the first time. Augmented reflexes faltering against chaos they were never meant to harness.

Eira hesitates—not fear exactly, but something close enough to rattle even her machine mind: doubt creeping into mirror-polished eyes.

"Almost there..." Ceige breathes it out like prayer or curse, her hands moving faster than thought across flickering keys while lines of code scroll past too quickly for comprehension now—a gambler playing blind against stacked odds.

Sweat beads on her brow despite cold sharp enough to bite through skin and bone alike as she works with nothing left but instinct keeping her alive.

Almost there...

Sloane spins.

Snow spits from her heels, white dust rising into the storm. She veers out of Eira's path, a streak of motion too fluid to be human.

"Catch me if you can," she says. Her voice cuts through the howl of the wind, thrown back like offhanded debris. Eira takes the bait. She lunges—and stumbles. A hesitation, a falter, her systems misfiring under the strain.

The storm rages above it all—tearing with icy claws, lightning splitting the sky into violent, jagged fragments. The world flashes white and dark and white again. Ceige hears none of it. None but Sloane's laugh, a sound like steel dragged across bone.

Laughter that says death is nothing to fear.

"All those bio-mods," Sloane calls over her shoulder, the words slicing sharper than knives, "and this is what you bring me? Desperation doesn't suit you, Eira."

She pivots again—graceful, effortless—as Eira barrels forward. Another feint. Another slip in precision that throws Eira off balance by inches but feels like miles.

"Must sting," Sloane says, voice laced with poison, "knowing you're just a second-rate killer wrapped in borrowed flesh."

The X-9 hums under Ceige's fingertips. Low at first—a vibration crawling up her arm—and then louder, sharper. Systems locking into place. Everything sharpens in her view.

"There." The word barely breaks against the wind, soft as breath after surfacing from drowning.

Sloane sees it first: hesitation flashing across Eira like a crack through glass. The fault line where perfection used to live.

Eira strikes—but not cleanly anymore. Just shy of landing, her missed blow skims air instead of bone. Millimeters off yet catastrophic in someone else's eyes.

Sloane smiles then—no, grins—a terrible thing full of teeth and hunger and victory waiting to be claimed.

"What's wrong?" she purrs as she moves closer now—faster now—striking where fractures run deep. "Premium parts starting to give out already?"

Eira stumbles again.

A flicker in the storm—a blink too slow for what she needs to survive—and Sloane is on her before she can recover.

Eira's kicks blur with inhuman speed but miss their mark by fractions that might as well be miles in the fight they're fighting now. Precision crumbles under pressure, slipping away like snow melting down mountainsides.

Sweat slicks synthetic seams where steel meets skin—a meld breaking at every fragile boundary. Her retinal display flickers; shadows crawl over her face like cracks spidering through porcelain once flawless but now failing under strain.

"You know what your problem is?" Sloane whispers through the chaos as she sidesteps a wild strike meant for her throat—a swing that pulls Eira forward into empty space instead of connection.

"You thought upgrades made you invincible."

She drives an elbow upward into Eira's ribs—not hard but precise—impact shuddering through metal plating that should've held firm and doesn't.

The machine that killed Cass without mercy—the weapon that was flawless—is fraying now at every edge that matters.

Circuits glitching.

Reflexes lagging.

Broken by seconds too small to count but just big enough to kill her.

Eira fires.

A plasma bolt sears into the crumbling ferrocrete beside Sloane. Neon chaos ripples across her mirrored eyes—fractured reflections flickering like a broken screen. Her overlays sputter, lines of light fraying into darkness.

"Hurts, doesn't it?" Sloane's voice is low, bitter. Frostbite in her tone. "Being trapped in a body you can't trust anymore."

The words hit like shrapnel.

Eira falters. Her precision shatters into erratic flailing, each movement jagged, desperate. Neural amplifications blink—on, off—leaving her stranded in the gaps between. The weapon she once believed herself to be splinters before their eyes. Not invincible. Not unstoppable. Just human enough to break.

"Now!" Ceige's shout cuts the air like a blade.

Her finger slams the X-9's command key. A bass hum pulses through the rooftop as Eira jerks—spasmodic, unnatural—a puppet yanked by invisible strings. Light threads her spine in one last blaze before dimming, sputtering like dying embers against cold wind. Her expression twists, raw and exposed; those mirrored eyes widen for the first time—not with calculation but with shock.

Sloane twists away from an errant shot's heat grazing her shoulder. A sneer tugs at her mouth, sharp and cruel as steel. "What's wrong?" she taunts over the din of the storm. "Systems overheating?"

Chaos spirals around them—neon flashes and howling wind—but Ceige doesn't waver. She watches Eira unravel, piece by piece, the moment fragile and electric: a live wire snapping.

"Back off!" Ceige commands, her voice cutting clean through the storm as she steps between them.

Eira stumbles backward, limbs jerking out of sync—stuttering like corrupted code failing its final execution. Panic bleeds across her porcelain face in fragments while gravity pulls at her inch by inch.

Rain-slick concrete betrays her footing. Arms flail wildly; legs skid without purchase. The growl rattling in Ceige's throat is low and feral—disbelief tangled with triumph—as Eira teeters on the edge.

The rooftop holds its breath.

A sharp whine slips past Eira's lips—a sound more machine than human—before she plunges into open air.

Sloane doesn't speak at first, just moves instinctively toward the ledge, drawn forward despite herself. "Shit," she mutters finally, hoarse and hollow as if the word itself might steady her shaking breath.

Below them, Eira vanishes into Cryosium's shadowed depths—her fall swallowed by storm-torn skies and jagged steel horizons.

Lightning splits the heavens above them.

Sloane stands silhouetted against it, rain licking down her face as she stares into the void below—the place where Eira disappeared along with all her cruelty, all her fire.

And beside her, Ceige watches silently, the moment heavy between them.

"She's gone," Ceige says. The wind snatches the words, tumbles them into the thunder.

Sloane doesn't answer. Just a shift in her shoulders—a tremor that might be relief, might be the weight of what justice demanded.

The towers rise around them, stabbing through storm clouds like jagged blades. Silent witnesses. Cold and unyielding, just like the city they keep watch over.

Sloane turns, her face carved in the electric light of the storm. Ceige catches something in her eyes—something sharp, something final. She won't understand it until tomorrow.

For now there is only this: the storm fading to silence, victory ringing hollow, and the fragile knowledge that somewhere, at last, Cass can sleep.

Chapter 11

The loading dock door slammed shut behind them.

Chaos severed.

They stepped into Cryosium's frozen maw, its breath sharp, cruel, indifferent. The ground beneath them was hard but lifeless, as if even the earth itself had given up.

"I think I love the earth," Sloane murmured. Her voice floated, light and brittle—a splinter of humor masking something darker.

Ceige didn't answer. Her eyes narrowed against the storm's fury, her expression carved from stone. Only her focus moved—flintlike, ready to cut through whatever stood in their way. Ahead, a faint glimmer—a fire barrel winking against the white abyss.

A promise of warmth.

A sign of life.

"This way." Her words came clipped and cold, a blade meant only for survival.

Her steps were deliberate, each one measured against the toll the ice demanded. The wind raged, feral and unrelenting, clawing at her like it wanted to drag her down into Cryosium's frozen grave. But Ceige didn't falter. This city had worked her like iron in a forge, hammering her into something honed, unyielding—a weapon forged for moments just like this.

Behind her, Sloane faltered.

Ceige caught it—the sway in her steps, the crack in her rhythm. That swagger Sloane carried so recklessly was gone, stripped away by some unseen weight. Fatigue? Pain? The knowledge coiled tight in Ceige's gut whispered louder now—she'd seen this before. Seen people unravel one breath at a time until there was nothing left but silence and regret.

"We stop," she said, cutting through the wind's howl with the finality of a command.

Sloane's laugh rasped out—a thin thread stretched too tight. "Did I hear that right? Ceige Rivers calling for a break? This must be the end of days."

The words might've drawn a smirk once—but not here. Not now. Ceige turned sharply on instinct, ready to snap back, but stopped cold.

Sloane had always been chaos in motion—green eyes sparking with rebellion, wild curls defying order itself. But now? Now she was ash where fire should've been. Her skin shone waxen under a sheen that wasn't just melted snow; it was something colder, deadlier—something hollow enough to swallow her whole.

"Don't," Ceige growled low as she moved toward her partner, unease curling hot in her chest like an ember fighting for air. "Don't give me *that* bullshit." Her words fell heavier than the snow around them.

Up close, Sloane looked worse. Exhaustion bled off her in waves—radiating like heat from dying coals—and whatever spark she once carried flickered faintly now, too fragile to trust against Cryosium's hunger.

She tried to grin—a crooked thing as weak as the storm's distant light. "Nice to know your bedside manner still sucks," Sloane said through cracked teeth.

Her body betrayed her lie. She wavered under its weight; whatever mask she'd worn shattered on impact.

"I'm fine," she whispered vehemently into the cold. "Just... Just need a second." But Ceige could see it: even seconds were running out fast.

This wasn't supposed to happen.

Not like this.

Get in, get the evidence on Eiskorp, kill Eira Halstead, get out clean. A plan honed sharp as a blade, hammered into Ceige's mind through endless drills and endless nights. Unbreakable. Unshakable.

All according to plan.

But Cryosium doesn't care about plans. Cryosium feeds on chaos.

Nothing here bends to will or reason. Nothing here ever goes right.

"Keep moving," Ceige orders at last, her voice brittle with frost and finality, leaving no room for doubt or argument. "We make it to that fire first—then we figure it out."

The flame flickers in the distance, faint and wavering, more mirage than beacon. Snow drifts rise like the walls of a labyrinth, swallowing their steps with each stride forward. Each step brings dread—not a creeping unease but something feral and ravenous, gnawing at Ceige's gut. Something whispering: *The fire won't save you.* Something screaming: *You're running straight into ruin.*

And then it happens.

Sloane collapses beside her—a sudden lurch, a stagger turned sideways—and doubles over as a cough tears itself from her chest. It rips through the howling wind like a blade through thin skin. And then blood—dark streaks on white snow, stark and damning as words scrawled across ice in some forgotten language of failure.

Ceige stares at it—stares too long—until it feels like staring into herself instead of the crimson stains pooling between their feet. Failure presses down on her ribs, tightens around her throat until she can't breathe right: failure to protect...what? A partner? A rival? A lover? The lines between those things had blurred long before this moment—blurred beyond recognition now in the vast whiteness of Cryosium.

Fuck.

Ice floods Ceige's veins—not water but razors—and cuts deeper than any wind ever could in this frozen wasteland. The sound of it—the howling shriek through jagged peaks—is nothing compared to the silence inside her head as she forces herself to breathe again. Forces herself to calculate; forces herself to shove *feeling* into some dark corner where it can't touch her anymore.

"How bad is it?" Her voice doesn't crack; doesn't waver; doesn't betray the fear crawling beneath her skin.

Sloane tries to smile, but it feels colder than the storm around them—brittle as ice underfoot before it splinters apart altogether.

"Cumaná," she rasps at last, every word broken by coughing fits that scatter blood like petals across snowdrifts. "Remember when I said I had it under control?"

"And you nearly bled out in a dumpster," Ceige snaps back without thinking, heat rising so fast it burns against the numbing cold of their surroundings. Her stomach twists itself into knots sharp enough to double her over if she let them—but she doesn't.

Her mouth hardens into something between a grimace and a snarl as she mutters: "Hell."

Before she can say anything else—before either of them can think beyond surviving the next second—Sloane's legs give way completely beneath her, crumpling like steel buckling under pressure too great to bear.

Ceige lunges forward without hesitation, instinct pulling harder than gravity as she catches Sloane mid-fall. They hit the ground together in an explosion of snow and cold that slices through fabric and flesh alike without mercy.

The heat comes next—not fire but blood slicking across Ceige's hands when they come away from Sloane's body smeared red in places where red has no right to be.

"Not...according to plan," Sloane murmurs faintly—each word evaporating like steam against Cryosium's icy air even as she struggles to form them.

Every breath sounds stolen.

Every second feels borrowed.

And Cryosium watches both debts mount higher still with unblinking indifference.

Words fail her now.

Her fingers move on instinct—delving through torn fabric, pressing into ruined flesh. The wound yawns open beneath her hands, dark and jagged. Too deep. Too far gone. Even Sloane's stubbornness won't keep this together. Blood seeps sluggishly, thick as spilled oil. Wrong color. Wrong everything.

"Damn it," Ceige mutters, a hiss slipping from clenched teeth, curses exhaled like smoke in the frozen air.

"You reckless idiot." The reprimand cuts sharp, though her voice fractures mid-sentence. Her words tremble under the weight of something heavier than anger.

Sloane exhales—a sound that might be a laugh if agony didn't hollow it out. "Didn't want to ruin... whatever this is." Her lips twitch upward at the corners, faint and faltering. Her face is bone-pale, shadows pooling under her eyes like bruises.

Ceige presses harder on the wound, desperate to stem an endless tide with trembling hands. But it's no use. The truth carves through her like a blade—there's no fixing this. Not here. Not now.

The thought settles over her like falling snow, cold and silent.

"Always so dramatic," she mutters bitterly, more to herself than Sloane. As if sarcasm could steady shaking hands or stitch torn muscle back together by sheer force of will. Her voice quivers anyway—splintering at its edges, breaking where she can't hold it firm enough. "You really couldn't let me end this clean? One uncomplicated exit... that's all I asked."

A faint smile ghosts across Sloane's lips—it flickers, fragile as frost in morning light. "Your bedside manner... sucks worse than before." The words scrape out unevenly before they dissolve into a wet, rattling cough.

Ceige freezes—just for a moment—but in Cryosium's unforgiving cold, even seconds drag long enough to hurt. Then she moves again, hands working with frantic purpose born less of hope than defiance.

"No one asked you to critique my people skills," she murmurs low and hollow as she wrestles against inevitability.

But defiance has limits.

So does blood.

"Ceige." Her name drifts out in a whisper so faint the wind tries to steal it away before it lands.

"Save your strength." Ceige doesn't look up. She keeps pressure steady against failing flesh—a useless act she cannot abandon.

Sloane's lips quirk again—a wry smile stained crimson at its edges. "I love you," she breathes, voice weak but unbroken despite everything. "You emotionally constipated asshole."

Love hangs there between them—a fragile thread stretched thin against the cold.

And then it snaps.

The words hit Ceige.

A blade, a jagged edge.

Sharp, unrelenting.

She stumbles, caught in the weight of Sloane's confession. The cold cuts into her lungs, her breath hitching against the frozen air. Her hands shake—are they trembling from the cold or from the impact? She doesn't know. "Goddammit, Sloane," she mutters, the words scraped raw, barely pulled from her throat. Ice clings to her face—it could be snow, it could be tears. Maybe both. "Why now? Why didn't you tell me before?"

Sloane's eyes soften. There's still that glint—faint but alive—of something reckless, something like mischief curling beneath the pain. "Time's funny," she says, so quiet that even the dying wind nearly swallows it whole. "It's never on your side." Her hand rises, unsteady, the pale fingers brushing Ceige's face like smoke—weightless, fleeting—but it scorches like fire. A touch that says everything words can't. "Didn't want to screw this up," Sloane adds, her voice thinning like frost melting under sunlight. "Happy endings... not really in the cards for us."

Ceige tilts into the touch despite herself. Despite the ache in her chest pulling her apart piece by piece. She feels unmoored, untethered, adrift—not in this snowstorm but in something colder still. "And now?" The question fractures as it leaves her lips. Her voice wavers, cracks wide open on the verge of breaking completely. "Now that you're—" The rest collapses under its own weight as grief floods in and chokes it off.

Sloane smiles faintly at that—if you could call it a smile at all. It's a flicker of defiance ghosting over her lips, brittle and fading fast. "Better late than never," she whispers through breaths shallow as a winter breeze. Saying it takes something from her—it costs too much—but she says it anyway. "Besides... I always thought I'd go out with style."

Ceige doesn't answer.

Not with words.

Not this time.

She just stares at Sloane like she's never seen her before—like she's peeling back layers of disguise and finally seeing what was always there beneath them all along. And in those final moments between them—those last fragile gulps of air—something sharp and clear locks into place: a bond forged too late to change anything.

"I—" Ceige starts to speak but falters when Sloane shakes her head gently, silencing her with nothing more than a look.

"Turns out," Sloane murmurs past breaths that scrape more shallowly with each passing second, "you don't pick who you fall for." Her mouth quirks just slightly—a flicker of dry humor breaking through grim inevitability like light through cracked glass. "Not in this shitty world."

The wind dies.

The snow stops.

The city holds its breath—a stillness falling over everything as if time itself had paused to listen.

Sloane's breathing falters too: shallower now, fleeting as a whisper carried on frost-bitten air. Then fainter still.

Ceige holds Sloane close.

Too close. Closer than she's ever dared before, as though sheer will might anchor Sloane to this world, keep her tethered despite the pull of inevitability. Her fingers knot in Sloane's hair, rough and desperate, like they're trying to fight nature itself. Her voice, when it comes, is low—stripped bare. Raw. "Don't you fucking dare leave me."

The words snap like a whip but fall soft, just a breathless plea.

Sloane's eyes flicker open one last time. That smirk quirks her lips—it's faint, barely there, but still defiant in the face of death. Irritatingly so. Eternally so. "Sorry... love," she murmurs, voice faint as smoke curling up from dying embers. "Guess I'm off-script again..."

Her chest rises once more.

Falls.

Doesn't rise again.

Silence swallows Ceige whole.

"Damn you," she whispers at last. Her forehead presses against Sloane's cooling skin as something inside her buckles under its weight—cracks wide open for one sharp moment before the cold rushes in to seal it shut again. Her voice breaks once more, bitter now. "You always had to have the last word."

She straightens slowly, movements deliberate and controlled—too controlled—as if denying the fracture beneath her surface makes it less real. She lifts Sloane into her arms without faltering; carrying weight has never been hard for a Judex like her.

But this weight is different.

The snow crunches underfoot with every step toward Eiskorp's dark silhouette ahead—a jagged monument rising out of Cryosium's ice-bound desolation. Each step drags heavier.

Every Judex dreams of this—their names carved into the bloodied history of their last triumph—but dreams are lies told to stoke the fire inside frostbitten souls. And Cryosium doesn't burn; it only freezes deeper.

Ceige pauses at the edge of shadow and steel, breathing hard against the tight chains of cold wrapping around her like iron shackles. She lets herself feel it for just a second—not grief, not even rage—but the ache of inevitability pressing down like a boot on her throat.

"Fuck." The word scrapes out of her throat, more hiss than sound.

She props Sloane against the icy wall with hands that don't tremble—don't dare tremble—even as she arranges the body with care that feels like mockery. Setting Sloane's shoulders back against frost and steel feels wrong in ways that language can't touch. The frost bites at Ceige's fingertips, numbs them—but it can't reach the hollow expanding from her chest outward.

This wasn't how it was supposed to go down.

Not someone else's bullet.

Not someone else's choice.

Ceige stares past Sloane's still face into something vast and dark—an emptiness she can't fight back against no matter how hard she tries —and lets herself drown there for just a moment before dragging herself up for air.

"In another life..." She chokes on the words. They're jagged things ripped from something raw inside her throat that tastes like blood or ice or both. Her gloved hand brushes a stray lock of hair from Sloane's pale face with all the softness she has left in her—not much—and then more softly still: "Maybe we'd be something."

Her breath fogs silver between them before vanishing into Cryosium's endless void.

"Maybe somewhere out there we still get it," she says, quieter now—almost to herself. "A happy ending."

Her voice fades faster than frost melting under sunlight that will never come here.

Snow falls, soft and unrelenting.

White ash from a world gone cold.

Ceige rises slowly, as if the weight of her own body might break her. Every movement is deliberate, drained of all urgency. She stands over Sloane, jaw clenched tight enough to crack, eyes dry but glossed with what she won't let fall.

"Rest easy," she says at last, her voice trembling where it once held steady. "You maddening... impossible... beautiful disaster." The words hover in the air, fragile and fleeting, before dissolving into the frost of her breath. "I'll catch you in the next life," she adds, quieter now. "Try not to ruin it before I get there."

Above them, the storm begins to unravel—clouds splitting apart like old wounds to reveal Cryosium's jagged skyline. Steel and ice spires jut into the heavens, sharp against a sky that offers no solace. The city looms in silence, a monument to failure. A grave marker for what she's lost.

Ceige doesn't move right away. For one long moment, she is motionless—just another shape carved into the frozen backdrop. Then her body remembers its purpose and forces her on.

"This mess," she mutters under her breath, low and bitter. Her words crystallize in the biting air before vanishing altogether—like everything else ever does.

Fragments of memory flash through her mind like broken glass: Eira's name glowing on a directive; Sloane's crooked smirk after their kiss; Eiskorps' atrocities bleeding across black-market screens; and now this—the final entry in a story no one else dared to finish.

Her hand closes into a fist at her side, tight enough to burn from the cold, but she doesn't loosen it. Won't loosen it. Nothing matters now—not anymore.

"I should've known," she whispers, harsh and rasping as though each syllable scrapes against her throat. "Should've known better than to think anything changes here."

She reaches into her coat pocket and pulls out the small metal flash drive. The chill bites through even her glove as it rests in her palm—cold and leaden for something so small. Ceige stares at it for what feels like an eternity, almost daring it to spring alive, to scream confessions or answers or anything at all.

"All those lives." Her voice falters on the first word but gains ground as she speaks again. "All that pain." Each word feels heavier than the last as it breaks free from her mouth. "And for what? For this?"

The wind moans, a ghost's lament winding through Cryosium's dead streets. Ceige startles a laugh—jagged, brittle, the sound of glass splintering.

"You'd laugh," she mutters, glaring at the body crumpled at her feet. Sloane's body. "You'd *love* this. Me here, losing my shit, talking to your corpse."

Her shoulders sag under the weight of it all. Not just Sloane—not just her—but everything. Lies stacked like ice blocks, cracking under their own weight. Truths left to fester in the dark. Every step that led her here when she should've known better. When she did know better.

She looks at the flash drive in her hand—a tiny thing, but it weighs heavier than grief itself—and wonders about the secrets locked inside. The answers no one wants to hear. The leviathans too massive to kill. Futures soaked red but sold shiny and clean on promises of progress.

"What the hell am I supposed to do with you?" she whispers, and the wind almost swallows it whole. The drive rests in her palm, thin and sharp-edged, pressing faintly through her gloves like it might cut straight to bone. It isn't much to look at—just a lifeless little scrap of plastic and metal—but God, it's heavy enough to crush whatever scraps of faith she hadn't already burned.

"Burn them down?" she asks the drive like it'll answer her back. "Bring Eiskorps to its knees?" A bitter laugh scratches out of her throat before she can stop it. "Like taking out one monster would melt this fucking tomb."

She glances toward the fire barrel a few yards away, its flames snapping defiantly against Cryosium's frozen breath—a flicker of rebellion clawing for air in a city that ate defiance for breakfast.

Sloane was like that fire, Ceige thinks—angry and hungry and too damn relentless for her own good.

Her fingers turn the drive over and over again, numb from cold but still feeling its jagged edges bite faint impressions into the leather of her gloves. For all its unbearable weight, it feels fragile somehow now—like truth itself is brittle enough to break apart in her hands.

Her lips form one word against the storm: "Justice." The sound goes nowhere—eaten by the howling wind almost as soon as it leaves her mouth—but sticks bitter on her tongue all the same.

What a lie that is.

What a fucking joke.

Her hand trembles.

It betrays what the rest of her won't: hesitation.

The drive hovers above the fire, a fragile offering to the flames. Heat rises in waves, greedy fingers licking toward her skin. She feels its warmth—strange and unwelcome, foreign against the cold spreading in her chest.

"This is for you, Sloane," she whispers, her voice tight, stretched thin under the weight of it all. The next words cut sharper but fall heavier: "And for everyone else who matters."

Ceige lets go.

The drive vanishes into the fire's ravenous mouth. Plastic curls and blackens like a dying snake, spewing bitter smoke that claws at her throat, stings at her eyes. Metal glows for a heartbeat—no more—before surrendering to molten ruin.

"Not according to plan," she says. A dry murmur, almost a laugh, but not quite. There's no humor left. None that matters.

She stands there, watching until there's nothing—nothing but ash and ember swirling in Cryosium's frozen breath. No evidence. No redemption. Just loss burned clean.

The snow waits behind her, endless and pale under a sky bruised with twilight. Her shadow stretches long and lean against the wasteland beyond. The silence presses down, heavier than any weapon she's ever carried.

Each step grinds into untouched snow as she moves away from what might have been—a spark for something greater, something brighter—but wasn't. Instead, there's only this: regret's bitter weight holstered at her hip like steel she'll never shed. Her fingers brush the grip of her X-9 pistol—a weapon still warm from its last judgment, carrying choices that can't be undone.

She doesn't look back.

Cryosium looms around her, indifferent as always—a labyrinth of ice and steel where souls vanish like smoke and are just as easily forgotten. Behind her lies failure; ahead stretches uncertainty; all around is a city that neither mourns nor cares.

In her pocket, Sloane's lighter sits heavy and cold—a stone she can't put down.

The city marches on without pause or pity as Ceige fades into its crystalline void—a shadow swallowed by snow and silence once more. Footprints trail behind her—the only proof she existed at all—and even those will vanish when the storm takes them.

Ashes to ice.

Gone again.

www.ingramcontent.com/pod-product-compliance
Lightning Source LLC
Chambersburg PA
CBHW060440310726

48977CB00001B/268